PRAIS

"Part delicious dream, part nightmare, That Risen Snow is an aberrant fairytale that is just as much a horror story. Boley has a knack for dark comedy and witty prose, and he blends it with a nearly-hardboiled voice uncharacteristic of (and therefore pleasantly unique in) dark fantasy fiction. It's a story you'll want to tear ass through but will equally want to slow down for, so you can savor the prose."

—*Brady Allen, author of Back Roads & Frontal Lobes*

"In 1912, the Brothers Grimm published an old German fairy tale they titled Snow White. Little did they know that a guy named Rob Boley would come along a hundred years later to reveal the 'true' and adult story of Ms. White, or 'Snow' as she was known in real life… No one could have possibly foreseen what would become of Snow in the hands of a diabolical, maniacal imagination like Boley's… Such a nice boy… with such a fevered mind. Read this with the lights on and a baseball bat or shotgun handy… you're gonna be glad you did. This is a Snow White you ain't gonna find in the middle school library… Get it, read it, and try to keep the screaming down."

—*Les Edgerton, author of Hooked, Just Like That, and The Bitch*

"That Risen Snow and That Wicked Apple make a deliciously diabolical tale—part Walking Dead, part turned-on-its-ear fairy tale. Rob Boley strikes the perfect balance of depth, drama, and dark humor to keep readers devouring the pages and leave them hungering for more."

—*Linda Gerber, author of the Death by Bikini Mysteries*

that RISEN *snow*

*A SCARY TALE OF
SNOW WHITE & ZOMBIES*

Book One of the Scary Tales, a Killer Serial

Rob E. Boley

StoneGate Ink 2014
Boise ID 83713
http://www.stonegateink.com

First eBook Edition: 2014
First Print Edition: 2014

ISBN: 978-1-62482-109-7

Cover design by Cory Clubb
Layout design by Ross Burck – rossburck@gmail.com

The characters and events portrayed in this book are fictitious. Any similarity to a real person, living or dead, is coincidental and not intended by the author.

Published in the United States of America

StoneGate Ink is an imprint of StoneHouse Ink

STONEGATE ink

ALSO BY ROB E. BOLEY

Short Stories Appearing in Anthologies:
"Companion" in *Day Terrors*
"The Harm" in *Once Bitten – Never Die*
"Hungry Like the Moon" in *Best New Werewolf Tales*

*In loving memory of Steve Bates for giving
me and so many others the light to show the way.*

that RISEN snow

Chapter One

Grouchy

THE CURSED GIRL NAMED Snow has slept for many moons, but it's the dwarf renamed Grouchy who's been dreaming. Today, he fears his dream will die.

He stands now at the bottom of the grassy hill with his six dwarf companions, yet he has never felt more alone—even when he was trapped in the bowels of Planchette Prison. He hides his anger in clenched fists. When he opens his hands, his fingernails have cut bloody crescent moons into his palms.

"Happily ever after, my hairy ass," he says.

"Grouchy," Merry whispers, "the Prince will hear you."

Grouchy gestures rudely toward the Prince. "Balls."

"That's enough," Bones says—his first words to Grouchy since the night before. Unlike the younger dwarfs' high-pitched voices, the elder Bones' deep voice commands respect, even from Grouchy.

Prince Mikael strides up the hill toward Snow's bed, dead leaves crunching under his boots. Upon the hillside, birds twitter and woodland creatures chatter. The dew covering the grass sparkles like the diamonds in the mine.

Bones removes the Prince's gloves from his shoulder where the young Prince draped them moments before. The ocean-blue gloves match the Prince's cape and leather boots, so bright and clean compared to the dwarfs' mining gear. About halfway between the hill and the dwarf Collective's cottage, the Prince's horse, also clad in blue finery, whinnies and tugs half-heartedly against its rope.

Atop the hill, the Prince leans over Snow's silver bed. Grouchy can barely watch as the muscular human hoists the bed's glass lid onto the ground.

Blushful lifts his pickaxe over his burly shoulder. "What think you, Dim? Is he really Snow's true love?"

The mute Dim shrugs in response, rubs his palms together, and wiggles his fingers.

"What'd he say?" Grouchy says.

Bones nods. "He says our Snow has been asleep for too long."

On the hillside, the Prince runs his fingers through Snow's hair. He leans over to kiss her, to break her curse.

Grouchy spits. "He's human. A swob. And a royal at that. How can we trust him with all that they've done to dwarfs? Don't forget—that wench Queen Adara wants Snow dead. How do we know he isn't in league with her?"

Merry smiles. When doesn't he? "Well, the Prince struck me as a cordial gentleman."

"Well, he struck me as a damn—"

An unmanly scream from the hill interrupts Grouchy's insult. The Prince struggles with something atop Snow's bed. Grouchy cranes his neck to see, but the bed topples to the ground, taking Snow and the Prince with it.

Grouchy yanks his rock chisel out of his boot and charges up the hill.

Above, birds fill the sky like a thick dash of pepper blocking the sun—all fleeing as if their feathery asses were on fire. In the periphery of Grouchy's vision, the assembled foxes, chipmunks, raccoons, and other critters scamper into the woods.

When Grouchy reaches the hilltop, the Prince is straddling Snow and pinning her shoulders to the ground. She flails beneath him, her faded yellow dress and periwinkle corset now stained with grass.

"Well, I'll be cored," Bones says from behind Grouchy.

"Leave her be, ass-muffin." Grouchy slams the blunt end of his chisel into the Prince's head with a dull *thump*.

At the same time, Snow lunges upward and bites a generous hunk of flesh away from the Prince's cheek. He jerks backward and clutches the wound, blood spilling between his fingers.

Grouchy's broken heart trembles in his chest. He tackles the Prince onto the slippery grass, and the human gasps under his weight. When he looks to see if Snow is okay, Bones is standing over her with an outstretched hand. Except Bones' bearded mouth falls open.

The Prince's gloves spill from his hands and clap limply together in the grass.

Grouchy hoists himself to his feet to get an eyeful of his blood-splattered Snowflake. Her eyes—usually sky blue—are now black pupils floating in twin pools of blood. Her lips twist in a sneer. She spits out the Prince's flesh, bares her teeth at them, and hisses. Without further warning, she lunges at Bones and buries her snarling face into the crook of his neck.

When Snow jerks her head away, strands of Bones' beard stick to her blood-smeared face. The elder dwarf collapses with a grunt. Grouchy shakes his head. The old witch with the apple lied.

Snow came back, but she didn't come back right.

Chapter Two

Grouchy

SNOW LUNGES AT GROUCHY, her face contorted into a mask of manic rage. She—his Snowflake—slams into his chest, knocking him to the grass and slapping the wind out of his lungs. She hisses. Her breath stinks of blood and rotten spices. He forces her back with a forearm wedged under her chin, even though he's yearned for those lips to touch his skin.

From behind, Blushful and Snoozy grab Snow's shoulders, and Grouchy scurries from beneath her. Merry plops onto Snow's back and her hands claw thick clumps of dirt and grass out of the ground. What the hells?

"Careful," Grouchy says. "That hag's curse runs deeper than we thought."

Coughy kneels next to Snow. "She's gone rabid." He inspects his hands with wide eyes. "I hope it's not contagious."

Bones and the Prince twitch, then their heads snap upward. Their eyes smolder crimson red like Snow's.

Well, shit. Grouchy sprints to the bed's lid—a domed iron frame with clear panes. Dim's a step ahead of him. Together, the two dwarfs lift the lid, their stout legs trembling. They charge at Bones and the Prince, slam into them with the lid, and pin them to the ground. Bones and the Prince throw themselves against the inside of the lid, now smeared with blood. Batshit. Completely batshit.

The dwarfs built Snow's bed with wheels so that they could bring her outside each morning onto the hilltop. Otherwise, the woodland animals—foxes, bunnies, and squirrels—would gather outside their cottage in vast numbers. Before the bed, it had taken the dwarfs a whole morning to clean the shit off of the lawn and an afternoon to scrape the birdshit off of the roof. The dwarfs later crafted the iron lid for the bed to prevent the animals from snuggling with Snow. Or worse. His Snowflake always did have a way with animals.

With his free hand, Dim pats his mouth twice, makes a claw sign, and wiggles his fingers over his arm.

"Blush, you see that?" Grouchy says.

"He said that whatever's wrong with them comes from getting bit."

Coughy scoots away from Snow and groans.

"Coughy," Grouchy says. "Rope."

"From the mine?"

"The Prince's horse."

Moaning, Coughy runs down the hill.

The Prince and Bones flail repeatedly against the lid, so that the glass panes seem to simmer. Already, Grouchy's muscles ache.

"Balls," he says. "We can't keep this up."

"If we put Snow under the lid," Blushful says, "they'll all be in one place."

"That's not bad, Blush."

When Coughy returns with the rope, Merry binds Snow's hands

behind her back and secures rope between her teeth and around her head. Grouchy's stomach boils seeing anyone touch his Snowflake, especially Merry.

Grouchy and Dim lift the lid slightly, then slam it down onto Bones' and the Prince's heads. While the rabid fiends are stunned, they lift the lid enough that Blushful and Snoozy can roll Snow underneath.

With all three batshits safely beneath the lid, the six dwarfs sit on the thick glass.

"This is a temporary solution at best," Coughy says. Whiner.

Merry pats the lid and smiles. "I think we came up with a wonderful solution given our limited time and resources."

Grouchy clenches his teeth. "Shut up. Just shut. The hells. Up."

Sweat drips from his forehead and splashes onto the glass panes. On the other side of the glass, the Prince's once-perfect nose now points to the left. Bones' shattered lenses are embedded in his plump cheeks. Snow's teeth worry at the rope, and her gums bleed. She twists her hands free. Figures. Merry can't knot for shit. A comb juts out at an improbable angle from her mangled nest of hair.

Only yestereve, Grouchy ran that comb through his Snowflake's raven locks. Ever since Snow ate that wicked apple, he'd ended every workday by washing the mining filth off his hands and face, changing clothes, and combing her hair. He'd told her stories and described the animals that visited the cottage. She always had a way with animals.

The rabid trio pummels the lid and jostles the dwarfs above. Droplets of saliva and blood splatter the inside of the lid.

"What now?" Blushful asks.

Grouchy grunts. "We can't hurt Snow. This ain't her fault."

"Or Bones," Blushful says.

"Or the Prince," Merry says. "Remember, his kiss awoke Snow

from her curse. He's her true love."

"Remind me to fumping thank him."

Damn this Prince to hells' puddles. Everything was fine until he came along with his good looks, fancy stitches, honey-gum, and princely posture. Fumping ass-pit.

When Prince Mikael of the Western Kingdom arrived earlier that morning, he told the dwarfs that he'd befriended a maiden named Snow last spring in the Eastern capital of Platessa, but that she'd disappeared. Towering over them, the Prince lovingly described Snow as he chewed his sweet-smelling honey-gum. Grouchy stared upward, neck aching, and tears brewed in his eyes. He clenched his hands into fists as hard as diamonds.

Now, the Prince shatters one of the glass panes. The dwarfs scatter to evade his grasp, and the lid rises.

"They're too strong," Snoozy says. "Tearing my roots." His red-rimmed eyes seem to squirm inside his skull. Typical. Snoozy always looks like sour death until Bones gives him his morning treatment outside the mine.

The Prince breaks another pane with a distinctive sneeze of glass. Again the dwarfs shuffle out of his grasp. They're running out of safe handholds.

"What are we going to do?" Coughy whines.

Hells with this. Grouchy stares down at the Prince and sees not just the object of Snow's affection but also destroyed dwarf villages, widowed dwarf women, orphaned dwarf babies, and hobbled dwarf men. He sees starving townships and crowded prisons, haunted pasts and lifeless futures. Worst of all, he imagines Snow embracing this pompous bastard. With a trembling hand, Grouchy pulls out his rock chisel.

The Prince lunges upward, and Grouchy thrusts his chisel into the young man's heart. Rusty metal pierces muscle and clicks against bone. He can't ignore how satisfying the impact feels. Thick blood spurts out of the wound, and the Prince collapses in a heap.

"Grouchy," Merry yells.

Grouchy shrugs. "That should make things easier."

Except it doesn't. Snow and Bones pound against the lid—now slippery with the Prince's blood—with the ferocity of a thunderstorm. More panes shatter.

"This isn't working," Coughy says.

"Agreed," Snoozy says. "Pretty red weeds." As usual, his head's full of oats.

"The cottage," Grouchy yells. "Now."

In unison, the dwarfs shove the lid one last time and knock Bones and Snow to the ground. Dim leads the dwarfs down the hill toward the cottage, their wide feet slapping at the ground. The lid crashes behind them, but Grouchy dares not look back. Soon, raspy breaths and rapid footsteps close in. The portly Merry lags behind, so Grouchy grabs his arm and pulls him along. They pass the Prince's horse, and the beast struggles against its rope.

First to the cottage, Dim holds the door open while the others rush in. Grouchy shoves Merry inside but stops just short of the threshold. He's never heard a horse scream before, and the sound sours his stomach.

Snow clings to the horse's side and bites its thick neck. It kicks and wails, a heart-wrenching noise that sputters seemingly without end. When the horse collapses, Snow tears open its belly. Her arms shove elbow-deep inside, ripping out organs.

Bones tries running past the horse but trips over its intestines. Snow's head snaps upward, sending a splatter of gristle into the air. She and Bones scramble to their feet and charge toward the cottage. She slips in the horse gore, spills to the ground, but lurches back up.

Grouchy slams the door. Seconds later, Snow thuds against it, hissing and grunting.

Merry clears his throat. "She always did have a way with animals."

Chapter Three

Grouchy

SNOW AND BONES THROW themselves against the front and back doors, respectively, but both doors were built thick enough to withstand attacks from the bears that roam the surrounding forest. Still, the pounding resonates through the entire cottage and causes the pots and skillets hanging in the kitchen to tremble as if with fear.

"We're doomed," Coughy says.

"Shut up." Grouchy rubs his temples and takes a deep breath of the cottage's familiar scent of old wood, fresh bread, and dwarf sweat. Is it his imagination, or does Snow's flowery aroma linger, too?

Coughy continues. "We're *ghunlichen*. We're too young to handle . . ." He wags his hands at the front and back doors. ". . . whatever this is."

Saying no more, he runs to the kitchen and scrubs his hands in the sink. Nearby, Snoozy stands on the counter, rummaging through Bones' herbs. Grouchy makes a mental note to keep an eye on Snoozy. Prison taught Grouchy how to spot someone with impure intentions—a skill necessary to survive those dangerous tunnels. Today, Snoozy's intentions appear anything but pure.

"They'll kill themselves if we don't subdue them," Grouchy says.

Merry flails his hands. "Subdue them? We're safe in here. No, we stay in the cottage."

The dwarfs' cottage is made of wood, chopped mostly by Blushful from the nearby hillside and constructed by Bones, Grouchy, Blushful, and Dim. Snoozy and Coughy helped a bit as well, and Merry delegated a great deal. The first floor is one lodge-style room divided by furniture into a wide foyer at the front, a sitting area with couches and a fireplace at the rear, a cramped kitchen on one side, and dining area on the other. In the cottage's center, a wooden staircase spirals upward to the second floor loft used as sleeping quarters. With its open space and dark wood, the cottage resembles a large underground cavern. Heavy shutters cover the few windows to block out light. Snoozy's and Dim's artwork decorates the walls, resembling the large murals painted by dwarfs so long ago in sacred caves.

The Collective's cottage is located in the easternmost portion of the humans' Eastern Kingdom, a region generally known as East-East. Here, the mountains scrape the sky. The rivers are silver knives carving the earth. The forests are thick and dark. The dwarfs' home is in just such a forest, and no road leads here. Rather, on the other side of the nearest mountain, the Slithering River flows almost a half-day's journey to the nearest town, a sleepy lumberjack village called Abundance. The village doctor is rumored to have knowledge of magic.

"We must take them to Dr. Killington in Abundance," Grouchy says. He hates the idea that they need help from a human, but Snow's safety trumps hatred.

Merry shakes his head. "He couldn't help her when she was asleep. What makes you think he can help her now that she's biting and hissing like a rabid cat?"

The rotund dwarf's pronunciation is too distinct, too crisp—like a member of the higher dwarf families who turned against their fellow dwarfs in exchange for scraps of power and privilege from humans. His father's probably a mayor or prison chief—a far cry from Grouchy's own father.

"Killington said to come if Snow's condition changed. I'd call this a big damn change."

"They're vicious monsters, Grouchy. Whatever curse has afflicted them, for all we know, it'll run its course by sunset. We have no business capturing them."

"Would you do nothing, you ass? Sit with our toes up our butts and rub each other's gemstones?"

"We need to remain calm," Merry says, now fiddling with that damn lucky rock of his. "Our first priority should be—"

Grouchy cuts him off. "Dim, what say you?"

Dim chews on his unlit pipe and stares at Grouchy. He is leaner and taller than the other dwarfs, and also hairless except for fuzzy eyebrows. He holds out two cupped hands, then turns them sideways to spill out the imaginary contents. He claps his empty hands together, then spreads them apart, palms down.

"What'd he say, Blush?"

Blushful scratches his thick beard. "He says he's not sure."

Dim arches an eyebrow at Blushful, who shrugs in response.

Merry crosses his arms. "Clearly, we need a leader."

"None of us are old enough to lead," Coughy says, returning from the kitchen—hands now an angry red from scrubbing.

"Balls," Grouchy shouts at Merry. "You want a damn election while our batshit friends outside bash down our doors?"

Merry shakes his head and smiles. "A simple vote will do. The Collective needs leadership."

"You?"

"Of course. I'm the oldest of the *ghunlichen*, and the most qualified."

Ghunlichen translates roughly from the outlawed dwarf tongue as "ancient child." Dwarfs can live well over a century, though their lifespans have dropped considerably since the humans carried out the Purge—the forced resettlement of the dwarfs to the Dwarflands, a flat and waterlogged wasteland. While dwarfs reach adult stature within their first two decades of life, as *ghunlichen* they spend the next two to three decades in prolonged adolescence. Gradually, their beards lighten until they're as white as Bones' beard.

Merry continues. "Plus, I'm the one Bones recruited first. I'm the one Bones gave the most responsibilities."

Grouchy scoffs. "He gave you busy work, you bird's ass. Fooled you into thinking you were worth a damn."

Cheeks flushed, Blushful puts a hand on Grouchy's belly. "Now isn't the time."

Merry's smile quivers. "So long as we're taking a hard look at ourselves, let's talk about what you just did."

"What?"

"You murdered the Prince."

"It was him or us."

"Did you stop to think about the consequences? If word gets out that a dwarf killed a royal? You might've started the next Rice War, you thug. Your chisel could hardly wait to dig into Prince Mikael's heart. And looking for what? Perhaps the object of Snow's affections?"

Anger hardens Grouchy's face. He lunges at Merry with tight fists.

Blushful and Dim wedge themselves between the two dwarfs.

"That's enough, you two," Blushful says, a hand on Grouchy's chest.

Merry's voice cracks. "I, for one, don't wish to be led by this criminal."

Grouchy puts his hand over Blushful's. "Who said I wanted to be leader?"

"You don't?" Merry's eyes narrow.

He shakes his head. "I vote for Blushful. He's strong. He's calm in a crisis. He's the only one left who understands Dim's hand-talking." Plus, he generally agrees with Grouchy on most things.

"Grouchy, I don't want—"

Grouchy cuts Blushful off. "That's why you deserve it, Blush, you don't want it. True leaders accept power, not yearn for it." He raises a hand. "I vote for Blushful. Anyone else?"

Coughy and Dim raise their hands. Snoozy stumbles into the room, eyes bleary, and raises his hand, too.

Grouchy smiles at Merry. "There. We have a leader."

Blushful shakes his head. "Okay, fellas. Let's capture our friends."

The morning wears on.

As Snow and Bones' pounding at the doors slows to a simmer, the dwarfs gather anything that can be used as a weapon or armor. Blushful asks Grouchy to help him with the drape upstairs, and he follows Blushful to the winding staircase.

It wasn't all that long ago—just last spring—that he followed Bones up these same steps to meet Snow for the first time.

———— • ◆ • ————

THE DWARFS RETURNED HOME after a long day's work in the mine to find that someone had picked the lock on the cottage's front door. Food scraps, dirty knives, and scattered dishes cluttered the kitchen. A pot of stew simmered on the stove, infusing the cottage with the warm scent of beef, vegetables, and exotic spices.

They ventured upstairs. Bones stood at the bedroom door, clutching a knife stinking of onions. Behind him, Grouchy hefted an iron skillet smelling of well-seasoned meat. The others carried spoons and bowls of stew.

Bones opened the door a head's width, revealing a room as dark as a moonless night. Grouchy followed Bones inside and banged his knee on something hard.

"Balls," Grouchy yelled.

Normally, the dwarfs' beds were spaced evenly throughout the room, but someone had pushed them together in the room's center to make one giant bed. That someone answered Grouchy's profanity with a shrill scream. Grouchy leapt toward the noise, swung his pan in a wild arc, and struck something soft.

"Shit," yelled a young woman's voice.

Bones lit his lantern, which revealed a wide-eyed human girl in a crumpled dress. Grouchy stepped back in awe. Her skin was as white as whipped cream. Her hair was as black as coffee. Her full lips as red as licorice. She sat on the beds, clutching her chest.

After a moment, Grouchy recovered from his shock. A human was dirtying his bed, invading his sanctuary. A damn swob here in the cottage. He clenched his teeth hard enough that his jaw ached.

Bones broke the silence. "Are you alright, ma'am?"

"I'm swell, except for my bruised tit."

Bones apologized and guided her downstairs to the dining table. There, she introduced herself as Snow and told her story while the dwarfs devoured bowls of stew.

Days prior, a man named Devere had taken Snow from the capital city of Platessa into the woods. He was her best friend Lox's father, as well as Queen Adara's Head Huntsman. She described him as very tall, with a bushy mustache. One of his ears had a split lobe from an archery incident. Deep in the wilderness, he had taken out his bow and shot an elk. He'd told her that the Queen had ordered her death. He'd dressed the elk, then sent her into the woods with some meat and told her never to return.

"I wandered for days," Snow said. "This morning, I stumbled on your cottage. Now please, may I go?"

"Just give us a moment, ma'am," Bones said.

Snow retreated to the couch while the dwarfs remained crowded around the dining table.

"Well," Bones said, "what should we do with her?"

Coughy held up his bowl. "Have her make more stew."

Dim nodded his head in agreement and licked his lips.

Grouchy's cheeks warmed. How could his fellow dwarfs allow this human swob to be here? Had they forgotten all that the humans had done to them, all the indignities and suffering?

"I don't trust her," Merry said. "Really, what are the odds that she would find this place? For all we know, she's a human spy."

"I've told you," Bones said, "King Francis knows that we're here. We have an arrangement."

"All the same, I vote she goes."

"For once," Grouchy said, "I agree with smiles here. She's only going to make life more difficult for us. Bad enough we're damn dwarfs living on human land. We've all heard the rumors about Queen Adara. What do you think she'd do if she found us harboring a fugitive? She'd decorate her walls with our hides."

"I disagree," Blushful said, his cheeks flushed the color of a red grape. "I think taking her in is the right thing to do."

Bones nodded. "My young friends, the Collective is an open community. All decisions are put to a vote. But remember that not long ago each of you was an outcast. And you've all dealt with your own horrors. You needed a safe haven, and you found it here. Now, who votes for her to stay?"

Bones lifted his own hand. Dim and Blushful—then the others—were quick to do likewise. Only Grouchy kept his hands crossed over his belly.

"Women. No fumping good will come from this."

———— ◆ ————

NOW, AT THE TOP of the stairs, Grouchy enters the sleeping room.

A cavernous loft with only one window carved into the front wall, it smells of dust and must. A thick drape over the window obscures most sunlight—all the better for their sensitive eyes. All seven beds are pushed together, just as Snow arranged them so many moons ago.

Even after Snow had eaten the apple, the dwarfs continued sleeping downstairs. No one had the heart to move the beds back.

Blushful grabs the drape. "Brace yourself."

Grouchy nods, and Blushful yanks the drape down. Outside, churning clouds mute most of the sunlight. The sun hasn't shined since Snow awoke. Below, she gnaws on a horse leg, now stripped to the bone. Viscera and blood coat her face and hands. Her comb juts out from her tangled hair, now matted with gore.

"Her beautiful hair." Grouchy rubs his eyes. "All those evenings I spent alone with her. The temptation was terrible."

"Grouchy, you don't—"

"Her true love's kiss. A damn kiss, Blush. That would have cured her. I told myself a thousand times that my love was true." He sighs. "But I never had the courage to kiss her. Was too afraid it wouldn't work. Now I wonder if maybe that shit-heel Prince wasn't her true love."

These words flow thick over his tongue. Since Snow's arrival, he has withdrawn from Blushful and the other dwarfs. Not that he was ever very social to begin with.

Blushful pats Grouchy's belly. "I have something to tell you, Grouchy. Something I didn't want to mention in front of the others."

Grouchy nods. *Crap.*

"Earlier, when you asked Dim which plan—doing nothing or capturing Snow and Bones—he thought was better, my translation wasn't entirely correct. What Dim really said was that it doesn't matter. Whichever we choose, we're likely doomed."

"Balls." Grouchy considers. "That's a kick in the rubies, ain't it?"

Chapter Four

Dim

SOME DAYS—ESPECIALLY TODAY—Dim resents his heightened senses.

Snow and Bones' intermittent hammering at the front and rear doors makes his brain throb. Their raspy hissing grates like a rusty blade scraped over leather, but what's loudest is the silence left by Bones. The elder dwarf was a mouth breather, and his breath whistled between his whiskers—a noise that always reminded Dim of a mouse wiggling its nose.

When Blushful and Grouchy return from upstairs, Grouchy wraps strips of drape around Dim—makeshift padding. Grouchy smokes his pipe as he works. Though Dim usually enjoys the smoldering scent, it smells foreign here in the cottage. Still, it almost masks the stink of dried gore from outside.

"Must you smoke that in here?" Merry says.

"Would you prefer I step outside, smiles?" Grouchy returns his attention to Dim. "Just the drapes? No armor?"

Dim shrugs, holds up a hand, and finger-sprints through the air.

It'll only slow me down.

Grouchy's eyes narrow. "Maybe you figure you might as well get it over with."

Ah, so Blushful told Grouchy what Dim had really said earlier.

Grouchy pats Dim's belly. "You'd be surprised what a dwarf can survive."

Dim nods. It was hard to say what terrible things Grouchy survived in Planchette Prison.

Grouchy holds up his tobacco pouch. "Join me for a smoke?"

Dim shakes his head and smiles. He's the only dwarf besides Grouchy who keeps a pipe, but he never smokes his. No, his pipe serves as a reminder of the terrible debt he owes.

Awhile later, the six dwarfs stand over the dining table—a round cross-section of an evergreen tree—and enjoy a quick snack. Ring after ring, the tree's long life ripples from its core at the table's center. The scents of cheese, venison, and seasoned bread with sunbutter and tomato sauce permeate the cottage. The dwarfs' beards—except for Dim, who has no beard, and Snoozy, who isn't eating—are heavily dusted with crumbs. Dim pops a cracker into his mouth. His disfigured tongue tastes only the slightest hint of the rich sunbutter, but his nose savors the scent. He swallows and rubs his meager belly.

Blushful pops a cracker piled with meat and cheese into his mouth and clears his throat. "We have three teams. Dim and I will duck out the kitchen window. Merry and Coughy, you'll make a ruckus at the back door to aggravate Bones."

"Perfect job for you," Grouchy says around a mouthful of bread.

"What'd I do?" Coughy says, munching on an apple.

"Wasn't talking about you."

"That's enough, Grouchy. You and Snoozy distract Snow at the front, so that Dim and I can unlock the shed, get the gem sacks, and head to the front door. We'll bag Snow first, then Bones."

Snoozy stares at the ceiling and works his jaw. He's chewing something, but not swallowing. Dim doesn't know the extent of Snoozy's horrors, but he worries that Snoozy is not dealing well with the day's troubles.

Horrors was Bones' term for the problems that plagued each of them. Some of the dwarfs have obvious horrors, such as Grouchy's quick temper, Blushful's shy anxiety, Merry's depression, or Coughy's fear of illness. Snoozy's horrors remain a mystery to Dim, but whatever horrors haunt Snoozy are somehow linked to the herbs Bones gave him each morning.

Bones forbade the dwarfs from discussing their pasts with each other. Instead, he met privately with them—their *alone time*, he called it—on a rotating basis each evening to discuss their horrors. Except Bones never discussed Dim's horrors. Indeed, Dim wasn't sure if he had horrors, other than the fact that he was physically different from the others. In fact, sometimes he felt like he was there to hear about Bones' horrors.

Coughy's voice dissipates Dim's thoughts. "Are we sure the gem sacks will hold?"

Dim nods to the group. The strong sacks, made of thick burlap, are used to transport gems downriver to Abundance.

"May your heart be empty," Blushful says to Grouchy, as they grasp hands.

"May your belly be full," Grouchy answers.

Dim slides his hands into Grouchy's pants pockets, empty except for his warm pipe and tobacco pouch. For practice, he switches the tobacco to the left pocket and the pipe to the right. Grouchy's oblivious.

It's been ages since he dipped a pocket. That life is over. After today, he fears that this life at the Collective will be over, too.

Grouchy offers Dim a hand. "May your head be empty."

He rubs a hand over his own belly. *May your belly be full.*

The other dwarfs take their places at the front and back doors, leaving Dim and Blushful in the kitchen.

"Key?"

Dim pulls out the shed's metal key. Bones has the only other copy. He pockets it and hoists his satchel over his shoulder.

"I'll go first," Blushful says, his high voice cracking more than usual.

They climb onto the counter and perch over the sink. At the front door, Grouchy bangs a fire poker and shouts obscenities. Snoozy clangs two spoons together, a surprisingly pleasant melody. At the backdoor, Merry and Coughy make a similar ruckus.

He unbolts the wooden shutters and opens the window. He's braced for harsh sunlight, but streaky clouds fill the sky with drab grays and bruised purples. Odd. This morning, the morning dew, wind direction, and bird songs indicated a sunny day.

He takes this as a bad omen.

Blushful drops into the bushes below. Dim pauses, listens, and follows. Outside, it smells of crisp leaves, mud, horseshit, and death. Dead leaves scurry across the ground. The bushes surrounding this side of the cottage hide Dim and Blushful well.

"You'll think me a fool," Blushful whispers, "but I feel more comfortable out here with those . . . with Bones and Snow, than I did in there. I'm just not cut out for—"

Something reaches through the bushes and grabs Blushful from behind. Impossible. No living thing can get this close to Dim without him sensing it. The attacker comes into view, and his stomach clenches.

It's the Prince.

His skin is pale. His lips are blue. He stares at Blushful with dull yellow eyes. His sheathed sword dangles uselessly from his waist. Blackish blood oozes from his torn face and chest. He stinks of death.

The Prince lunges at Blushful's neck, but the dwarf grabs his chin. The Prince chomps down with a grunt, severing two of Blushful's fingers. Twin sprays of blood arc through the air across Dim's chest.

"Argh," Blushful yells.

The noise jolts Dim. He jumps and grabs the windowsill, swings and kicks the Prince in the head. Dim pulls Blushful away. The Prince shuffles forward, moans. Dim's senses don't lie.

The Prince is dead.

Walking dead.

The corpse reaches for Dim, but he ducks and shoves it into the bushes. He spins around to check Blushful, steeling himself in case his friend's infected. But the wounded dwarf just stares vacantly at his bleeding hand.

The Prince lurches out of the bushes.

Dim punches the Prince between the legs. No effect. He kicks the back of one knee. It falters. With a grunt, Blushful finally intercedes and hurls the Prince into the bushes. Dim snatches the Prince's ornate sword from its sheath as the undead human flies through the air.

Blushful collapses.

Time is short. Dim pushes Blushful under the window. He covers his own eyes, then finger-walks. *Walking dead.* Next, he points to Blushful, then upward. Himself, then upward. *You go first. I'll follow.*

Blushful nods and steps onto Dim's interlaced fingers. He hoists Blushful upward with a mute grunt. Already, Blushful's skin is clammy.

From the bushes, the Prince moans. Blushful pulls himself through the window, and Dim passes him the Prince's sky blue sword. He's about to pull himself up, but hears the footsteps too late.

A feverishly hot hand grabs his neck, then teeth clamp into his shoulder. It's Bones. His rapid breaths rustle the whiskers around his lips. Like an angry mouse wiggling its nose.

Dim tries to scream, but can't.

Chapter Five

Grouchy

GROUCHY BANGS A FIRE poker against the front door, each blow jarring his finger bones. His Snowflake responds with hissing and thumping until her onslaught abruptly stops. Next to him, Snoozy continues drumming spoons on the wood with an irritatingly pleasant rhythm.

He touches Snoozy's belly. "Something's wrong."

They listen.

Silence.

Grouchy sprints to the kitchen window, just as Blushful spills through the frame. His right hand, now missing two fingers, sprays dark blood over the walls.

Blushful yells Dim's name.

What follows is chaos.

Snoozy jogs into the room, sees Blushful's wound, and promptly vomits. Blushful again yells, "Dim." Snow's blood-crusted face appears in the window. She grabs for Blushful, but Grouchy yanks him away and slams the shutters in Snow's face.

He steps backward, slips in Snoozy's mess, and lands flat on his back. Vomit splashes, stinking of sour bile. Snoozy giggles, and Grouchy hears only the snide laughter of his captors in Planchette Prison. The noise becomes a lit match dropped into Grouchy's belly. There, his anger explodes. He shoves Snoozy into the dining table. Merry—smiling like an idiot—wedges himself between Grouchy and Snoozy.

Over Merry's shoulder, Grouchy watches Coughy approach Blushful and hand him a towel. Blushful nods, wraps the towel over his hand. With Blushful unaware, Coughy raises a kitchen knife.

Grouchy shouts Coughy's name, shoves Merry aside, and tackles the knife-wielding dwarf. They topple sideways into the counter, and the blade clangs to the floor. Before Coughy can react, Grouchy tucks him into a headlock—forearm wedged into his throat. Coughy gasps.

Merry kneels over Blushful.

"Careful, Merry," Coughy rasps.

"What the hells, Cough?" Grouchy flexes his forearm.

Coughy sputters, "He's been bitten."

"Looks fine to me."

Blushful pushes Merry away. "I'm in no way fine, but I'm not one of those things." He gestures toward the window. "Not yet. Grouchy, let Coughy go."

Grouchy relaxes his arm. Coughy falls to his knees and rubs his throat. Across the kitchen, Snoozy leans against the counter, his jaw constantly working. What is he chewing? The kitchen stinks of puke. Grouchy pulls off his stained padding and sits. His back throbs from the fall.

"Blush, what in the bear's bouncing balls happened?"

Blushful explains how the Prince attacked him and Dim. "Dim helped me through the window and gave me the Prince's sword."

Blushful points at the blue blade, speckled with blood, now lying on the kitchen counter. Its ornate, twisted handle reminds Grouchy of a frozen river. "Then Bones grabbed Dim. Bit him. He's dead. Or one of them."

"And then there were five." Grouchy shakes his head. "But how? The Prince is dead."

Nobody speaks. Outside, Snow and Bones claw and pound against the doors and window. The Prince moans.

Blushful clears his throat. "Last thing Dim said was, 'Walking dead.' If he said the Prince was walking dead, I believe him."

"How can a dead body walk without a soul?" Merry says.

Coughy shrugs. "Who says humans have souls?"

"They do." Grouchy shoots Coughy an eyeful of stink. "They do."

Blushful turns to Coughy. "If Dim pushed me in here, he thought I was safe. He wouldn't endanger you."

Coughy lowers his eyes, wipes his nose. "How does the wound feel?"

Blushful considers his finger stumps. "Damnedest thing. Doesn't hurt at all. It's numb."

"Shit," Grouchy says. "We need a new plan."

"No, we don't," Coughy says, his voice rough as sandpaper. "This isn't a project. This isn't like digging a hole. We're in the hole. You have to see this thing for what it is: a disease." Coughy stands. "Magic or no, it's a disease. It is spread by biting, so bodily fluids are the carrier. We must assume that any fluid—blood, saliva, sweat, piss, tears—can infect. The infection has two phases, what we'll call hot and cold. In the hot phase, the infected are wild and frenzied—at their most dangerous. If they're killed in the hot phase, like the Prince, they enter the cold phase. They keep coming. We have no reason to believe they'll ever stop." He points at Blushful.

"He was bitten by a cold infected. We must assume that he'll turn, too, eventually. We must restrain him, just in case."

Blushful waves wearily, trembles. "Fine. Just give me a blanket."

Coughy continues. "Dr. Killington may be able to cure this disease, but our first step is containing it."

"No." Grouchy points a stubby finger at Snoozy. "Our first step is watching pukey-pants here clean up his damn mess."

Coughy ignores Grouchy. "The longer the infected run free out there, the more the disease spreads."

"Can we not call them 'the infected'?" Grouchy says.

"Horrors," Merry says, again rubbing his black stone. "We'll call them Horrors."

The dwarfs exchange a look. Grouchy hates it when Merry makes a good suggestion. Still, *Horrors*. Bones would appreciate that.

He nods. "So where the hells do we contain these Horrors?"

Coughy rubs his throat. "We let them in here."

Chapter Six

Coughy

"WE LET *THEM* IN *here*?" Merry's smile wobbles. "Are you joking?"

Coughy shakes his head and winces at his sore neck. "We let them in, and then barricade ourselves upstairs and secure the cottage doors from the outside. With them trapped in here, we go to Abundance to fetch Dr. Killington. Better to bring him here than bring them to him."

Grouchy nods. "It's doable, but it'll take time."

"It's worth a shot," Blushful says. Tainted blood seeps through his bandage. Sour sweat beads on his forehead. Disease is saturating Coughy's friend.

"The cottage is our sole asset," Merry says. "We can survive in here for days. Let's think this through."

"We don't have time," Coughy says. "This is no normal disease, Merry. It's a plague.

Plague.

The word sends a chill through the cottage, just as Coughy

intends. The Plague decimated the Dwarflands in the wake of the Purge and the subsequent Rice Wars. After the Purge, the humans disbanded the ancient tribes, imprisoned the chiefs, mixed populations from different tribes into random townships, and installed new dwarf leaders—swob puppets. They forced dwarfs to plant and harvest rice, then ship the bulk of the crop to the human kingdoms. The dwarfs' new, spiritually bankrupt life caused many of them to take pilgrimages to their sacred caves in their former homeland, now the Ascendio Kingdom. This led to a predatory practice called grinding, in which swobs charged dwarfs admission to enter the caves, blocked the entrance once the dwarfs were inside, and then left the dwarfs to starve to death. But all that paled in comparison to the Plague, which killed thousands of dwarfs.

Merry points at Blushful. "What about him?"

Coughy can barely look at Blushful. Filth. Blood. Sweat. Snot. Disease. Misery. "Restrain him," Coughy says. "Just to be sure."

Everyone clearly agrees, but nobody moves. No one but Snoozy, rocking back and forth and murmuring to himself.

Blushful grimaces. "Fine. Tie me to a chair. But you damn well best carry me upstairs before you let them in here."

"Hells." Grouchy pats Blushful's belly. "You're our bait."

Grouchy strips off his vomit-stained outer shirt, tosses it on the floor, and binds Blushful to the chair. All the while, Coughy eyes Grouchy's hand—the one that touched Blushful. Nastiness. Misery. Contamination. Coughy approaches and touches Blushful's shoulder with his fingertip. Cool as fruit.

"No hard feelings, Cough," says Blushful, his breath stinking of dead flowers.

Coughy nods. His fingertip throbs. Death. Pain.

Merry stands over them. "Can I help?"

"No offense, smiles," Grouchy says, "but your knots are shit."

Merry's smile only widens. "Ah. Yes. Anything we can do for you, Blushful?"

Coughy speaks up. "Treat it like any other poisonous bite. Keep his hand above his heart to slow the blood flow from the wound. Blushful, stay calm. The slower your metabolism, the better. Merry, I need hot water and starfish oil. And raylee root to slow the infection."

Blushful's heavy eyes focus on him. "Thanks, Cough. Good thinking, containing the Horrors in here. You're good having around, when you're not trying to stab me."

Coughy laughs and wipes a tear from his eye. Not because it's funny. No, he's crying because only he knows what will happen after all the Horrors, including Blushful, are safely locked inside the cottage.

He's going to burn it to the ground.

Chapter Seven

Grouchy

GROUCHY RETIES BLUSHFUL'S ROPES so that his injured hand—now cool as autumn shade—is above his heart. The raised hand makes Blushful look like he's perpetually trying to get everyone's attention. Grouchy's about to say as much when Merry returns from the kitchen holding an empty jar.

"Isn't this where Bones kept the raylee root?" Merry says.

Coughy frowns and looks around the cottage. "Better question: where's Snoozy?"

Snoozy missing. Raylee root missing. Damn. Grouchy rises and notices a blade-shaped smear of blood on the counter.

"More better question," he says. "Where's the Prince's sword?"

Soon, Grouchy stands with Coughy and Merry below the staircase, a winding wooden structure with one thin railing circling its outer side. In the Collective's early days, Grouchy and Blushful built this staircase, cutting and finishing each step. Snoozy worked every night for a year carving designs on the railing. It's the core of the cottage, both literally and symbolically.

The door upstairs is shut, though Grouchy knows he left it open earlier.

"That raylee root could give Blushful extra hours to live," Coughy says. "Possibly days."

Grouchy puts a hand on the railing—smooth wood inlaid with ancient dwarf symbols. "What do you know about raylee root?"

"Bones was the expert," Coughy says, "but I do know it's mildly euphoric. Slows down the heart. It's often used to keep injured lumberjacks from going into shock. Or to slow poisons."

"So that's what Bones gave Snoozy every morning before we entered the mine?"

Merry bites his lip. Coughy wipes his nose.

"Shit-wickets," Grouchy says. "I know we don't talk about each other's horrors, but there's no point denying it. The damn rules have changed now."

"Why?" Merry says.

"What?"

Damn. Merry's wearing his speech face—furrowed brow, raised chin, thoughtful smile.

The portly dwarf holds out his hands. "Why must things change? We're still the Collective, with or without Bones. We should think hard before throwing out everything the Collective stands for. Everything Bones lived for."

"Lives for," Grouchy says. "He ain't dead yet."

"And odds are," Coughy says, "he'll still be walking even when he's dead."

"Why did Bones give Snoozy raylee root?"

Coughy shrugs. "It can be used to treat addiction. Usually for puddleweed smokers. In small doses, it's entirely safe. It keeps the smoker from getting the sickness when they quit their poison. It helps them to cleanse. To maintain."

Grouchy shakes his head. Treating poisons with poisons. That was Bones for you.

One of Bones' suggested anger treatments for him was vulgarity. Bones told him that he kept his hatred for humans and his anger in general bottled up inside, like a whistling tea kettle. And when Grouchy asked how to let out the pressure, Bones patted his belly and told him, "Shit, dwarf. Fumping cuss like all hells until your flaming mouth is raw, your core is wanked, and your ass is numb." They laughed long and hard over that.

Grouchy smiles now, thinking of Bones' nasal laugh. Except his smile quickly fades when thinks about how he treated Bones last night. And now, he'll likely never get the chance to apologize.

"It's safe in small doses," Merry says. "What about larger doses?"

"It causes paranoia, hallucinations, and aggressive behavior."

"Shit," Grouchy says. "Let's get this over with. Coughy, wait down here in case he gets past us."

Grouchy and Merry climb the staircase, each armed with an iron skillet, rope, and an oven mitt. The stairs groan under their feet, a mumbled warning. Grouchy tries focusing on the task at hand, but Merry keeps blathering.

"Grouchy, I wanted to discuss a concern about Coughy's plan. If we trap Snow and Bones in this confined space, they might turn on each other. They're like wild animals. Who knows how they'll react in such close quarters."

Damn. Merry has a point. "Hadn't thought of that."

"I'd hate for something to happen to Snow. Bones is so much stronger. And who knows what the Prince is capable of, being dead and walking and all that."

Grouchy tries not to think about that spud kissing Snow, ruining his Snowflake. Biting Blushful. Grouchy's stomach quivers. He'll kill that shit-loaf again and again, until his royal highness stays dead.

"Merry, let's get the sword and herbs away from crazy Snoozy first, okay?"

The grinning dwarf nods.

Grouchy listens at the loft door. It's quiet, the calm before the storm. He knows this sensation well. Sometimes the storm's quick and violent, like at Planchette Prison, but that's not how it happened with his Snowflake.

No, she came on slow and steady.

———— ◆ ————

IT STARTED A FEW days after Snow's arrival. As usual, Grouchy was the first to awaken, and he stomped out to the outhouse. He slammed the door, dropped his pants, sat down, and winced. He had slept on the floor again, and his back was a bag full of jagged rocks. Someone knocked on the door.

"Can't a dwarf shit in peace?" he said.

"I'm terribly sorry," Snow said.

Grouchy winced. "I'm sorry, uh, miss. Just a moment."

Grouchy wiped himself slowly, trying to be quiet. Nothing to do about the smell, unfortunately.

He stepped out into the crisp air. Snow was sitting on a nearby log, the same one Grouchy and Bones used for their alone time. A bluebird stood on her hand, chirping a song.

"Tur-a-lee. Tur-a-lee."

Grouchy sat a respectable distance away—not wanting to smell her human stench—and pulled out his pipe, already stuffed with tobacco.

Already, the other dwarfs were falling all over each other to win the swob girl's favor. Even Bones helped Coughy make cologne with herbs found in the forest. They feared that the dwarfs' natural odor might offend her, since humans had better senses of taste and smell, while dwarfs had better sight and hearing. It was the dwarfs' blunted tongue, many humans joked, that caused them to be so thick around the middle. Dwarfs kept eating in hopes of eventually tasting something. Damn swobs.

He puffed his pipe. "The, uh, outhouse is free."

Snow waved her free hand. "I pissed in the woods."

"Oh. Well, fine."

"You have a beautiful home. Most homes make a wall between us and nature, but yours feels like a part of nature. Not apart from it."

"That was the idea," Grouchy said, then added quickly, "when I built it."

"You built it?" She raised her eyebrows. Even the bluebird chirped in appreciation.

"Well, yes. Er, the others helped."

"You must be great with your hands."

Blood rushed to Grouchy's cheeks. His stomach swelled. He pointed at the bluebird. "You've a way with critters."

"They've always liked me." Snow smiled. "You want to see something?" Grouchy nodded, and Snow whispered to the bird. "Go fly onto the roof."

And the bluebird did.

"They do whatever you tell them?"

"Usually."

"Just birds?"

"Birds, squirrels. Things with feather and fur listen well. Fish, snakes, lizards, they pay me no mind."

"Bet you can hunt some easy game."

"Oh, no." Snow shook her head. "I couldn't take advantage, not even for a meal."

"You a witch?" Rumor had it some swobs, mostly gypsies, had magical abilities.

Snow laughed. "I'm just a kitchen girl in King Francis' Chamber House."

"What's that?"

"It's where all the royals and politicians from the three kingdoms meet to eat fine meals, drink lots of wine, smoke petalweed, gossip about each other, fump each other, and occasionally govern."

"Ah."

She bit her lip. "I don't know why the animals understand me, but they do. Sometimes they talk back. I do them the courtesy of listening. Sometimes I even understand them."

"That's all most folks want. Someone to listen."

Snow nodded. "Could I puff your pipe?"

A swob smoking his pipe? Oh, hells no. Yet he handed it to her. She took several draws and exhaled brilliant smoke rings. The bluebird soared from the roof and flew in and out of the ever-widening rings.

"Sometimes I wish I could fly like a bird," Snow said, her voice so soft that Grouchy thought he was listening to her stomach.

Grouchy nodded. "Me too."

"Why would you fly?"

"Sometimes I get so angry." He lowered his gaze. "It sits all hot and heavy in my belly. It holds me down. If I could fly, I could just rise above it all. I could be free."

She nodded. "When I was little, I found a long-forgotten passage in the Chamber House that led to a circular courtyard sunk into the Bella Gardens. I'd sneak out when the other servants were sleeping—well before sunrise. I called the courtyard my Secret

Hole. In the spring and summer, the birds became my friends. I sang to them, and they sang to me. It used to pain me so when they flew west for the winter. Eventually, I realized that I could command them not to migrate. Sure, they froze to death, but at least I wasn't alone. Eventually I realized that I shouldn't stop them from leaving. I was the one who needed to leave, but I never did. Well, not of my own accord. I just wish I could be free. Wish I could stare at the sunset and follow it. Chase the sun. With nothing to stop me. Free."

The sun rose over the trees. Pink light illuminated Snow's pale flesh. She returned his pipe and he took a puff, momentarily tasting her kiss on the stem. Fruits and creams.

Despite himself, Grouchy, too, wanted to sing her a song.

———— • ◆ • ————

NOW, HE EASES OPEN the loft door.

It's dark inside, but it shouldn't be. The day grows late, but not that late. He looks back at Merry. "He knows we're out here and why we're coming in. This won't go easy. Stay here. Try to talk some sense into him. If anyone can get through to him, it's you."

With that, Grouchy kicks open the door and slides inside. Two mattresses cover the window. In the middle of the room, Snoozy has stacked the beds into a haphazard fort. Grouchy crouches low in the darkness and waits. Merry stands framed in the doorway's light, prattling on and on.

"Snoozy, old boy, do come on downstairs. We could certainly use your help. Let's have a nice pot of soup. Blushful's been asking for you. He really needs some of that raylee root that you've got. Not all of it, just—"

A blade glints. Footsteps sprint across the room at Merry. Grouchy slams his skillet upside Snoozy's head—a glancing blow that sends Snoozy and the sword clattering to the floor.

Backed onto the stairs, Merry's mouth hangs open. "He could have killed me."

Grouchy grabs the doorway. "He didn't."

"You used me as bait."

"Point is, he's down. Now, why don't you—"

Merry's eyes widen, focused behind Grouchy. Too late, he hears rapid footsteps. Snoozy slams into Grouchy's back, shoving him into Merry. All three dwarfs stumble onto the landing, collapse the stairwell's railing, and spill downward into open air.

Anything but free.

Grouchy's belly flip-flops as the dwarfs plummet in a chubby tangle of stubby limbs. Quick as a sneeze, they crash through the dining table. The impact slaps the air out of Grouchy's lungs, rendering him unable to utter the curse words most appropriate to the situation. His left knee flares with pain, as if demons were pounding a pickaxe into his joint. Under him, Merry moans and coughs.

Grouchy slides off of Merry's bulk, gasps for breath, and examines his leg. His jaw drops open, and his heart lurches. His knee and thigh are a mess of sticky blood and bone shards.

Fump. He's crippled.

Chapter Eight

Merry

MERRY GASPS FOR AIR as Grouchy rolls off of him. He trembles to his core, heart galloping behind his ribs. His lungs starve for air. Every limb aches to the bone. Finally, he's able to take a breath. He gulps at the air, grateful to be alive.

Nearby, Grouchy pounds on the broken table.

"Damn it to hells. Shit nuggets."

Tsk. Always such needless vulgarity. He sits up, stares at Grouchy's leg, now covered in tomato sauce and broken dishes—the remains of their meal left on the table.

"It's okay," Merry says. "It won't stain."

"What?"

"Lemon juice should get it out."

"What?" Grouchy stares at his leg, shakes his head, and grunts. A laugh erupts from his round belly. "Har!"

Merry jumps, but then starts laughing, too. The two dwarfs exchange looks and laugh some more. Warmth snuggles in Merry's belly. Before he joined the Collective, he never had moments like this. The other young dwarfs in his township shunned him because his father was the mayor. Even here, he's always been different than the others.

They continue laughing until Grouchy notices Coughy kneeling over Snoozy, who's apparently lifeless.

"Snooze," Grouchy says, scrambling over to see his fallen friend. "Is he dead?"

Coughy shakes his head. "Just unconscious. Hard to say how long before he wakes up. If ever. Look here." He uses a napkin to open Snoozy's lips, which are now neatly split down the middle. Blood seeps from the wounds. Snoozy's teeth and tongue are stained piss yellow.

"What the hells?"

"Can't say about the split lip. That's too clean to have come from the fall. But the yellow stains are from raylee root. He must have chewed quite a lot."

"Balls. Search his pockets. See if there's any left."

In one pocket, Merry finds a handful of gnarled roots, each as long as his hand. They feel like shriveled strips of leather and smell like sour dirt.

"Are either of you hurt?" Coughy asks.

"My knee," Grouchy says. "Feels like someone's mining for gems inside my leg."

Merry smiles. "You rest. I'll make the raylee root tea for Blushful."

Grouchy squints at Merry.

"It's the least I can do."

Finally, Grouchy nods.

Merry retreats to the kitchen, puts on the tea water, and pulls out his worry stone. Smooth and flat, it sits in his palm looking for all the world like a hole.

Bones gave Merry the worry stone early in the days of the Collective. At the time, Bones said, "You must be stronger than the darkness inside you, Merry. It is pliable. But with enduring effort, it can be beaten. Think of the river that cuts a canyon. The ant that builds a hill." He held out a rough black stone, its edges jagged and twisted. "Rub this."

And so Merry did. The edges bit into his thumb.

"It hurts, yes?" Bones said. "Don't let that stop you. Don't let pain or fear stop you. Keep rubbing, and you will mold that stone—that darkness—to your will."

He rubs the stone now, its surface smoothed over the years by Merry's tireless rubbing. And maybe a little sand-parchment. He studies Grouchy and Coughy from a distance. Coughy applies grapeseed ointment to Grouchy's knee and wraps it with cloth soaked in witchleaf oil. Which of them is strong enough to help him beat the darkness?

Coughy was ready to kill Blushful without hesitation. He's always been prone to worry, fearing that even the slightest cut would result in amputation, that every sneeze would blossom into an all-consuming fever. And now? To what lengths will Coughy go to protect himself from Snow's curse? No doubt about it. Coughy may be Merry's greatest ally—even if Coughy did concoct this foolish plan.

Assuming Snoozy wakes up, Merry still needs a third dwarf for a majority. That means he must enlist Grouchy. Or get rid of Blushful. His belly aches at the thought. He clenches his worry stone and listens to Grouchy and Coughy's discussion.

"Cough," Grouchy says, "about our plan, how do we know that Snow, Bones, Dim, and the Prince won't tear each other apart in here?"

"Good point." Coughy considers. "We gas them. Just like the

bear."

Years ago, a bear wandered into the mine overnight. Not wanting to force a confrontation, Bones mixed a potion that induced temporary slumber. The dwarfs wheeled the bear out of the mine on a mining cart. After that, the dwarfs erected a gate over the mine's entrance.

"Yes." Coughy nods. "That's perfect."

"Perfect hells. This is far from perfect. But can you make the sleep potion?"

Coughy pats Grouchy's belly. "I believe I can."

Grouchy raises his voice. "Merr, when the tea's done, pack up our supplies. Cough, you work on the sleeping potion. I'll rig the front and back doors so that we can open them from upstairs with a cord. I'll make some crossbars to reinforce the loft door. And we'll need rope to climb down and lock the Horrors in from outside."

Coughy joins Merry in the kitchen.

When Grouchy is out of earshot, Merry whispers to Coughy, "Are you sure about this? We're taking an awful risk by letting them in here."

Coughy rummages through the lower cabinets. "It's a much worse risk leaving those things out there."

"This cottage is our greatest asset, Cough." He forces himself to drop the final syllable off Coughy's name. "I'm worried that we're throwing that away. We don't know what'll happen if we just wait this thing out."

Coughy rises, eyes unflinching. "My whole family tried waiting out the Plague. We went into the swamps. We thought we could wait it out. We didn't know that it was already right there with us. You know who got sick first?"

Merry shakes his head.

"I did. It started with vomiting, followed by fevers and chills.

They could have abandoned me there in the swamp, but they didn't. Soon, the sickness took all of them. Everyone I ever cared for puked up the contents of their stomachs, then blood, then whatever was left inside. Their muscles twisted and contorted into unforgivable postures. Many bit off their own tongues. They went blind. Eardrums ruptured. Mother first. Then my sisters. Brother. Father. All reduced to screaming, bleeding, sweating, drooling masses of diseased flesh."

"I'm sorry." He tries patting Coughy's belly, but he jerks away.

The teakettle whistles harshly. Outside, the pounding on the doors intensifies in response. Merry sighs, removes the teakettle to a trivet, and grabs the tea pouch. Clearly, Coughy isn't on his side. It's possible he can sway Snoozy, maybe even Grouchy, but not if Blushful is still around.

He remembers his father's words. *"Sometimes you have to do terrible things for the greater good. That's what being a leader is all about."*

Merry tucks the raylee root into this pocket next to his worry stone and stuffs the tea pouch with other herbs. For the greater good.

For the Collective.

Chapter Nine

Grouchy

AT THE LOFT WINDOW, Grouchy secures a knotted rope to the windowsill. Outside, the earth takes its first nips at the setting sun. Snow paces in the front yard. Periodically, his Snowflake snarls and lunges at the door hard enough to make the windowsill tremble.

He will fix her. Or die trying.

There's no sign of Dim or Bones, but now the Prince stumbles into view, his skin pale and blotchy. His mouth hangs open, and a line of bloody drool spills down his chin. Grouchy remembers how it felt to stab the Prince—like he was getting revenge for all his ancestors. For all of the dwarfs now decaying in the ground. For all of the unborn dwarfs who will grow up poor and hungry. In that moment, he understood his father Kiel's rage and violence. Except stabbing the Prince didn't ease the anger smoldering in his belly. If anything, his belly burns hotter.

Snow rushes to the Prince, snarls, and sniffs his wounded neck. Grouchy grits his teeth.

"Hello," Merry says from behind him.

He jumps, then grunts. "You startled me, smiles."

"That's a first. I don't think I've ever scared you before." Merry drags a bag into the room—supplies for the journey to Abundance.

"Only when you start talking."

"Ah." Merry's smile wobbles. Never could take a joke.

His knee aching, Grouchy crosses the room, pats Merry's belly. "Only kidding. Y'know, for someone who smiles so damn much, you sure as hells take things too seriously."

Merry shrugs. "And you don't?"

Grouchy eyes Merry and grunts. "Blushful drink his tea like a good boy?"

"Yes. Yes, he did. I hope it helps him."

"I'm going downstairs. We're 'bout ready."

Grouchy checks first on his companions in the sitting area. Blushful dozes in his chair, and Snoozy still lies unconscious. He finds Coughy in the kitchen. Already, the cottage reeks of harsh vapors almost strong enough to mask the lingering scent of vomit and blood.

Holding a napkin over his mouth, Grouchy says, "The gas mixture almost ready?"

Coughy nods. "Just about."

Grouchy's anxious to get this done, to make his Snowflake better. She was always so tolerant of his impatience, even when he hovered over her—well, under her—in the kitchen.

Like the day she told him about King Francis.

———— ♦ ————

IT HAD BEEN ANOTHER long day in the mines. He was hungry, and Snow was still messing around in the damn kitchen. He was hungry, and Merry was prattling on about a better chore system. Furthermore, he was hungry.

"It doesn't matter if I'm done," she said. "The stew must be done. We must listen to our meal. Do you hear what it's saying?"

"Yeah. It says, 'Get me out of this pot and into Grouchy's belly.'"

Snow laughed and bonked Grouchy's head with her ladle. "No, silly. It's saying." She slowed and deepened her voice. "'My flavors are still intermingling. I need to simmer longer so they all can get to know each other. Also, I need more salt.'"

"More salt?" Grouchy handed her the salt shaker.

Snow shook the salt into her palm, then added it to the stew pinch by pinch. "Many a meal has found itself woefully underdressed with a shamefully revealing lack of salt." She sipped the stew. "I once met King Francis, you know. He traveled often, so it was rare to meet him in person. We were cooking that night—a grand dinner to celebrate his anniversary with Queen Adara. His sixth wife, if I remember correctly. His fifth was Adara's sister, you know. Anyway, he was limping around the Chamber House halls, trying to find the chamber pot. He was impressively drunk.

"He found me boiling water in the kitchen. As he pissed into a pot of soup, he pointed at my boiling water, ranting about how heat was just the, uh, articles? Particles? Barnacles?" She shook her head, ebony hair flowing like a dark river. "Whatever. He said that heat was just the essence of something moving faster and faster." Snow laughed. "It was very odd, but made a queer sort of sense. I imagine that's what's happening with our stew. All the ingredients are zipping around like hummingbirds, drinking each other's nectar. Isn't that lovely?"

Grouchy grunted. "Sounds like fairy tales."

"Yeah, but it's nice to think these particles exist. They certainly smell wonderful." She closed her eyes and smelled the stew, her face flushed from the heat. When she licked her lips, a deeper longing replaced the hunger in his belly.

———————◆◆———————

NOW, COUGHY CLEARS HIS throat and pats Grouchy's belly.

"You okay?" Coughy says.

He nods. "This is a good plan, Coughy. I think we're finally going to get ahead of this—"

"Uhhhrrr."

The moan comes from the sitting area. It must be Blushful. Grouchy and Coughy exchange wide-eyed stares.

They're too late.

Chapter Ten

Snoozy

SNOOZY'S MOUTH IS FULL of chalk. His stomach has twisted into a knot. His split lip throbs. His body feels like a bag full of uncooked rice. His bladder aches to the point of bursting.

The first thing he hears is someone—Snow?—pounding at the front door. Weight. Voices murmur in the kitchen, something about gas. Wait. The cottage stinks of alcohol—only stronger. Nearby, Blushful naps, tied to a chair with a bandaged hand bound over his shoulder. Wrapped. Rapt.

Snoozy tries processing these sights, sounds, and smells. When he closes his eyes, he sees flashes of blurred memory. Taking the raylee root from the cupboard. Cabinet. Running down the hill away from Snow into the cottage. Cabin net. Oh, hells. Bones. She bit Bones. Drumming on the door. Vomiting.

He sits up, and his stomach somersaults sluggishly. A vengeful rodent digs at the inside of his skull.

"Uhhhrrr," he moans.

Coughy and Grouchy run from the kitchen. Grouchy carries a

blue sword at the ready. When they see him, both smile and exhale deeply. Coughy kneels over Snoozy and pats his belly. Grouchy stares down at him and shakes his head. He vaguely remembers tackling Grouchy out of the loft.

"Are you okay?" Snoozy says.

Grouchy nudges his hip with a boot. "I'm fine. No damn thanks to you."

"Did I knock you off the stairs?"

Grouchy nods. "Yeah, but Merry broke my fall."

"Can you move your fingers and toes?" Coughy says.

Snoozy tries and finds that he can.

"What do you remember?" Coughy says.

Snoozy shakes his head, then clenches his forehead until the pain subsides. "Not much. Snow woke up all wrong. She bit the Prince and Bones. When we got back here, I was weak. I just wanted my treatment. Treat mint. What the tree meant. My raylee root. Bones hadn't given me my daily ration yet." Tears spill out of his eyes. Damn it. He came so far, only to start all over. "I found the jar and I took some. I took a lot. After that, everything's a daze."

"What happened to your lip?"

Snoozy touches his split lip and chuckles. He points at the sword in Grouchy's hands. "I thought the Prince's sword was a treat. A honey-stick."

"Good you didn't think it was a lass," Grouchy says. "You might've split worse than your lip."

Snoozy furrows his brow. "Upstairs, I thought I was in my tree. You know, the one out back." He refers to the oak tree where he sketches pictures and plays his flute. Hanging from its branches is Grouchy's punching bag. Snoozy long ago nailed handholds into the tree's trunk, dwarfs not being known for their climbing abilities. "Except it smelled like burnt applesauce. Applause. Bows. Boughs.

And the limbs were blazing. Burning." He can still see the tree in his mind. Smoldering. Swaying.

Grouchy leans over and pats Snoozy's belly. "Can you walk?"

He nods. "Yes."

"Good. Then you can help me get Blushful up the stairs."

"Okay. But first, I need to pee."

Grouchy points at the front closet. "Bucket's in there for that. For anything else, you know where the outhouse is."

Chapter Eleven

Blushful

THIS IS TORTURE.

Not the evil coursing through Blushful's veins. Not the cold empty hole swirling inside his belly. Not the fact that his best friend in the world, Dim, is now one of those monsters. No, torture is Grouchy and Snoozy staring down at him in his chair at the foot of the stairs—the center of attention.

"How you doing, Blush?" Grouchy says.

"Same as I was doing the last time you asked me. Like cold, hard crap."

"Yeah? Well, you smell like it, too. But I must be hungry for punishment, because me and Snoozy are gonna haul your sad sack up the stairs now."

Upstairs, Merry finishes packing supplies. Downstairs, Coughy makes final preparations in the kitchen—from which stinging fumes now emanate. Grouchy takes the lead, hoisting up Blushful's chair by the back while Snoozy lifts it by the legs.

With each lurching step, the hole in his belly yawns and bites his insides. His brain is a fried egg sloshing inside a broken shell. He breathes slowly, each inhalation punctuated by a stabbing pain in his lungs. His bones are carved ice, and his muscles are rice paper. His finger stumps tingle.

Halfway up the stairs, Snoozy speaks up. "Can't I do something else besides pull a cord? Huh. Accord. Acorn. Cored."

Blushful keeps his eyes on Grouchy, who now has the Prince's sword strapped to his back. Grouchy points upstairs. "I want you with Merry."

Blushful coughs. "Hey, you two. Less talking. More lifting."

"Hear that, Snoozy? Leadership's gone to his damned head."

His vision fades, like a candle flame in the wind.

Grouchy speaks in the darkness, his voice so distant. "I don't trust that grinning idiot. Keep an eye on him."

"I want you both to know," Snoozy says, "I'm sorry about what I did. About being so weak."

Blushful tries waving his hands, to warn them both. Except his joints freeze, his bones turn to ice.

Grouchy grunts. "Ain't none of us perfect, or we wouldn't be here." A pause. "What's wrong?"

"Blushful's gone hollow," Snoozy says.

"He breathing?"

Hot hands fumble with his face and neck. The voices are now distant pulses, the thump thump of sloshing blood. The hole in his belly explodes without warning. A flame ignites in Blushful's heart and bursts through his veins. The hands touching him are now icy cold.

When he opens his eyes, the world is blood reds, flame oranges, and aching yellows. A hiss erupts from his belly, now a squirming mess of hot coals.

The hole inside him burns unbearably.

Must be extinguished.
Doused in blood.

Chapter Twelve

Coughy

HISSSSS.

As soon as he hears the hiss, Coughy knows that Blushful has
turned. Damn. He hoped the raylee root would slow the infection.
He scrambles to cover the pot of flammable liquid on the kitchen
counter—a volatile blend of cooking oil, coal-oil, and lubricant—
not sleeping gas, but liquid explosive. Fumes sting his nose, even
through the napkin tied over his face.

He reaches for his lantern.

Hisssss.

The second hiss starts upstairs and finishes below with an
awesome crash.

Now on the ground floor, Blushful rises to his knees. The
remains of the chair hang by tangled ropes from his waist, arms, and
legs. Blood drips from his hand and his mouth, now a twisted snarl.
A sliver of bone juts out from his forearm through shredded muscle
and splotches of fat. His busted nose points sideways.

Blushful stands, and chair fragments clack together. The

shadows cast by Coughy's lantern tremble. The cottage and all its contents are as terrified as he is. He can't take his eyes off the drool and blood dripping from Blushful's sneer. Infection. Disease. Death.

Hisssss.

With a lurch, Blushful charges at Coughy. The terrified dwarf grabs a kitchen knife and drives the blade bone-deep into Blushful's shoulder. Sounds like flint striking stone.

Blushful doesn't notice. He shoves his face into Coughy's neck. He stinks of ointment, sweat, and spoiled food. Coughy pushes at Blushful, but teeth dig into his flesh and clink against clavicle.

The wound is a freshly struck match. Coughy shivers, first in revulsion, but then convulses involuntarily. He throws his head back and chokes on a scream. The lantern shatters on the counter.

He bumps against the pot filled with fire.

Grouchy and Snoozy run down the stairs.

It's only a matter of moments before the liquid explosion erupts.

"G-get away," Coughy sputters. "Get the hells—"

Hissssss.

This time, the hiss is caused by flame kissing vapor. The explosion screams in his ears, louder than any thunderstorm. In an agonizing flash, it hurls him and Blushful across the room. His body crunches into the wall, then rolls in a burning tangle across the floor. His back boils like a bubbling cauldron. For one blissful moment, everything goes black.

Far too soon, a terrible fire ignites within.

Chapter Thirteen

Grouchy

A GREAT BALL OF fire explodes in the kitchen. The cottage shakes, and the stairwell rattles. A hot, invisible hand shoves Grouchy onto his ass, knocking him halfway down the stairs.

Snoozy catches him before he tumbles off the staircase. Grouchy's injured knee throbs. The stink of burnt hair and smoke assaults his nose. The gruesome scene he just witnessed is branded inside his skull: Blushful's bone jutting out of his forearm like a bookmark, Coughy's wide, desperate eyes, and the almost lustful motion of Blushful's head slurping at Coughy's neck.

He assesses the madness below. In the kitchen, flames rejoice in an orgy of destruction. Across the cottage, Blushful rises, his beard charred. One arm hangs uselessly. Back in the kitchen, Snow perches on the charred windowsill, the shutters blown out by the explosion. Crusty brown blood covers her face and arms. Coughy, now in flames, staggers across the ground floor—spreading the fire.

In unison, Snow and Blushful charge the stairs. Snoozy pulls Grouchy to his feet, and they scamper up the staircase. Blushful leaps for Grouchy's foot, but thankfully loses his grip on the stairs. Snow jumps and scales the side of the stairs like an oversized spider.

Grouchy reaches the landing, but Snow grabs his ankle. He falls forward—stomach smacking against the wood floor—then rolls onto his back. Snow clambers onto him, her slight limbs jabbing the wind from his belly. She hisses, spraying blood and spittle. Before she can bite, footsteps hurry forward. Merry slams one of the supply bags into her chest, propelling her and the bag backward off the stairwell.

Coughing, Grouchy crawls into the loft. Merry slams the door behind him. As soon as he latches the crossbars, heavy thuds pound on the other side. The door rattles on its hinges, but the crossbars hold.

For now, they're safe. Flickering shadows lick across the three dwarfs' faces. The scratchy scent of smoke spreads in the still air.

"And then there were three," Grouchy says. "Shit."

Merry helpfully does the math. "There's more of them than us."

"We have to leave."

Merry shakes his head. "But where?"

"The mine." Grouchy unsheathes the Prince's sword, tosses it onto the bed. "We'll be safe there. If we trap them there, we can find Dr. Killington."

Merry shakes his head. "Trying to capture them is what got us into this mess. We need to protect ourselves."

Grouchy steps toward Merry. "Coward."

"Fool," Merry says. "We don't know that a cure exists. Do you think Bones would risk everything to save a horde of monsters?"

"Bones valued life. And freedom." Anger bubbles in Grouchy's belly, making his squeaky voice low and grumbly. "Those are our friends. They're prisoners in their own bodies."

"And you'd know all about being a prisoner, wouldn't you?"

"Bones knew the risks when he took Snow in. Knew he was defying the Queen."

Merry flails his hands. "And look where that got us! We need real leadership now. Please."

"I've got more leadership in my hairy ass than you have in—"

"Then why did Bones give me so many responsibilities? He was grooming me to take his place."

Smoke slithers under the door. Below, flames crackle and something crashes. He and Merry are close enough that Merry's breath grazes Grouchy's beard. Sweat pours down his back, soaking his clothes. They don't have time to argue, but Grouchy can't help himself.

"He gave you busy work to make you feel useful, you ass. Think about our names. I'm Grouchy because I'm a pissed-off, motherless fumper. Dim was Dim because people thought he was a dumb ass. Coughy was Coughy because he was frightened of a sneeze. Bones gave us names to help confront our horrors. Except for you. You he called 'Merry,' not because you're so fancy-fumping happy, but because you're so sad with your shit-eating grin. If you confronted your horrors head on, you'd shrivel like the dickless twerp that you are."

"You want to face things head on?" Merry says, voice high and cracking. "What about your feelings for Snow?"

Grouchy flinches, the word *Snow* like a slap in his face.

Snoozy steps between them and places a hand on each dwarf's belly. "Don't."

Merry continues. "You think just because Snow can talk to animals, she'd lower herself to loving a mongrel like—"

Rage bursts in Grouchy's belly, hotter even than the inferno raging below. He roars and lunges, ready to gouge out Merry's eyes, strangle him, crush his nose, and worse. Except Snoozy holds him back.

Eyes wide with fright, Merry grabs the sword from the bed. "Come on then. See what a coward I am."

"Enough." Snoozy shoves Grouchy, then stomps to the door and holds the crossbars. "Stop it, or I open this door."

Grouchy and Merry exchange agitated glares.

Snoozy coughs, smoke thickening around his ankles. "We are in a burning cottage filled with Horrors. Your argument can wait." Snoozy's eyes go glassy a moment. "Wait. Weight. Weightless. Sprouting inside. Patience. More patients." He shakes his head. "It's time to go. Now make your peace."

Grouchy coughs. "Snoozy, we don't need—"

Snoozy kicks the door. "I will open this door right now. Let all the nasty seeds inside."

Merry extends a hand to Grouchy. "Fine."

Grouchy takes Merry's hand, the palm smooth and soft. It's not a worker's hand. He considers giving Merry a painful squeeze, but decides to behave.

"May your hands be empty," Grouchy says.

"May your belly be full," Merry says.

Grouchy turns to Snoozy. "Grand. Now, can we go?"

Snoozy shakes his head. "You two go. I'm staying."

Chapter Fourteen

Grouchy

A THICK BLANKET OF smoke oozes under the door. Flames lick their hot tongues against the rafters under the floor. Sweat drops off Grouchy's nose and into his beard.

He shakes his head. "Don't be an ass-pit, Snooze."

Merry chimes in. "Snoozy, we need you."

Snoozy coughs. "They outnumber us. And they're fast. But if I stay here and distract them, you'll have a chance. Grouchy, you're the best fighter. And Merry's a great planner. Hells, he was probably right about waiting this out. Weighting it out. Pound for pound. On the door."

"Snoozy, focus."

"Right." Snoozy rattles his head. "Someone has to stay behind to distract them. You can't, because you couldn't outrace them to the mine on a bum leg. And Merry couldn't—"

Grouchy finishes for him. "Because he's a chunky butt."

Merry's smile folds into a pout. "Darn it, Grouchy."

Snoozy grins. "But I'm faster than both of you."

"Fine." Grouchy raises the Prince's sword. "You're taking the Honey-Stick."

Snoozy smiles wide, and blood oozes from his split lip. "It'd only slow me down. Besides, I don't know how to play it, but I wager you do."

Grouchy nods grudgingly. "Alright, but Merry and I are taking supplies for all three of us."

He lifts one of the bags and gasps at its weight—like a load of rocks. He drops it and yanks it open to reveal rope, hand tools, candle lanterns, and a medicine box. No. That idiot wouldn't have been so stupid. He ignores the pain stabbing his left knee and grabs another bag. Kitchen pots and silverware. Another. Blankets.

"Merry, where's the fumping food?"

Merry's grin quivers between chubby cheeks. "That must have been the bag I shoved at Snow."

"You packed all our food in one bag?"

"Well, yes. I wanted it organized. Food in one bag. Tools in one bag. Cookery in another. And so on."

"Cookery? And so on?" Grouchy turns to Snoozy. "Who's our great planner?"

Cursing, Grouchy shoves the supplies into two bags. Snoozy pounds on the door, putting the Horrors on the other side into a frenzy. Heat rises from the floorboards.

"Remember, Snoozy, this ain't no jackassed suicide," Grouchy says. "We need you."

Snoozy holds his hand out. "You'll get me soon enough."

Grouchy and Merry clasp Snoozy's hand.

"May your hearts be empty," Merry says.

Grouchy nods. "May your footprints be empty."

Snoozy squeezes their hands. "May your bellies be full."

Grouchy grabs the knotted rope and eases out the window. The nighttime air instantly cools his sweaty clothes. He shivers. With bare rope biting into his hands, he lowers himself to the ground by the front door, now battered and bloodstained. He squints. One of Snow's torn fingernails is embedded in a jagged gouge. Above, the full moon peeks from behind murky clouds loitering in the sky.

Merry reaches the ground next, and Grouchy shoves him toward the bushes. There, Merry's eyes go wide with fear. Grouchy turns around, and a tall shape lumbers forward.

The Prince.

By the moonlight, the undead bastard's skin is the color of moldy bread. Dried blood covers his chin and chest. His hands clench, popping terribly—already going stiff. Gritting his teeth, Grouchy tries unsheathing Honey-Stick, but the hilt snags on his bag.

The Prince grabs Grouchy's wrist—his grip strong and cold—and Grouchy's training takes over. He twists free and snaps the Prince's wrist. Unfazed, the Prince leans forward to bite Grouchy's face.

His breath smells like a rat's ass-pit.

The Prince's mouth jerks to a halt a thumb's length from Grouchy's cheek. A kitchen knife protrudes through his throat. Holding onto the knife's handle is . . . Merry. Huh. Imagine that.

Merry tries using the knife to pull the Prince backward, but the Prince struggles against the blade like a hooked fish. Finally, the sharp metal slices through his neck with a rubbery pop. The Prince's head, now supported by a third of a neck, plops to one side. His teeth gnash, chomping at air. Black blood slides lazily from his neck.

Enraged, Grouchy kicks the Prince to the ground and stabs Honey-Stick into his chest again and again—each wound a debt owed. For the dwarfs. For the Purge. For the fallen warriors.

For Snow.

Something crashes inside the cottage, near the window. Merry pulls him away, across the yard. No more time for revenge. The Prince is finished anyway.

At the head of the path, Grouchy looks back. The flames have completely engulfed the cottage's first floor. Their home is destroyed.

Damn it to the core.

As he and Merry run down the long path, Grouchy gulps at the chilled air. His feet pound the earth, each step hammering a rusted nail into his injured knee.

Bones purposely wanted the cottage built a distance from the mine. The walk provided a refreshing way to get the blood pumping each morning before work. Likewise, in the evenings the hike helped the dwarfs leave behind the stress of work.

What is normally a fine jaunt now becomes a terrifying sprint. The trees overhead cast eerie shadows over the uneven ground. The forest is as still and silent as a corpse. Just a few more steps to the last bend. Balls be bouncin', they're almost safe.

Until the bushes on the left rustle. Grouchy tries running past, but something heavy tackles him from behind. He sprawls to the ground, the wind knocked from his stomach. Just as he grabs Honey-Stick's handle, sharp teeth clamp into his left calf.

He hopes it's Snow.

Chapter Fifteen

Snoozy

FLAMES GNAW AT THE loft's floorboards. Horrors slam against the door, jarring Snoozy's mind. No patience. Know patients. Wood patients. Would puppets. Strings. Master. Mistress. Distress. This dress. A wedding. Wetting. Snow. Snow angels. Snow puppets.

The bitter taste of nothingness, like sour chalk, spreads down Snoozy's throat into his stomach. Emptiness festers under his fingernails, too, as if his bones are burrowing out of his flesh. Chewing the roots has left the inside of his mouth as dusty and hard as the bottom of a mineshaft. He can't stop grating his tongue against his teeth. He tastes coppery blood.

He spent years fighting off his personal horrors, and now he must start all over. Soon, his body will turn on him. The chills. The nausea. His muscles aching, his bones throbbing. Vomiting at both ends. It's too much.

He sees only one option out. But how? Hang himself with the rope dangling out the window? Deflated balloon. Slice his wrists and let the emptiness spill free? Bleeding seeds. No, his only redemption now is to go down fighting, maybe give Grouchy and Merry precious extra moments to reach the mine.

He picks up a weathered fire poker from the scattered supplies on the floor, the twisted iron offering a perfect grip. A torn sheet wrapped across his face helps filter the smoke. Next, he fastens rope to a split piece of wooden headboard—a shield. With a kitchen knife tucked into his pocket, he wipes sweat from his brow. Ready.

Wood groans as the Horrors thrash against the door. He inhales deeply. Smoke scratches his throat, and he coughs, then takes another breath.

Wait. Weight. Wait for it.

He pries the doorknob loose, so that the two crossbars are all that's keeping the door closed. He yanks off the lower bar, then loosens the top.

Thud. Thud. Thud.

Nails wiggle out of their holes as the Horrors continue their onslaught. Snoozy pulls the pins out of the hinges, and holds on to the door.

Thud. Thud.

The Horrors knock loose the top crossbar, shove the door inward. Sidestepping with the motion of the door, Snoozy slams heavy wood on top of them. Bones and Snow thud downward, sandwiched between door and floor. He scurries over them and onto the staircase, where Blushful emerges from a blanket of smoke. His beard is charred. One arm dangles—a mess of bone shards and torn muscle. The other arm reaches forward.

Snoozy smacks away Blushful's hand with his shield. He kicks Blushful backward off the staircase. The burnt and broken dwarf crashes below, hisses angrily.

Something clatters behind him. Snoozy pivots. Bones leaps, but Snoozy sidesteps and shoves Bones off the staircase. Bones grabs

Snoozy's hand—thankfully drenched in sweat—but loses his grip and topples below.

Too close.

As Snow appears in the doorway, Snoozy bounds downward three stairs at a time. Smoke, flames, and gnashing teeth surround him, but more important is what fills him—hunger. Not hunger for raylee root or apple whiskey or puddle weed, but hunger for life.

Fire consumes the furniture and walls. Flames crackle. Snoozy leaps off the stairs. Thick smoke blinds him, but he should have a clear shot to the back door.

A hand grabs his ankle. Blushful.

He topples onto his belly with a grunt. He smacks at Blushful's hand with the poker, then kicks his charred face. Blushful's nose and several teeth shatter. The Horror keeps coming. Snoozy stabs his knife downward through Blushful's wrist and into the floor, and then rolls away.

He's lost his bearings. He crawls across the hot floor, fully expecting teeth to latch onto his flesh at any moment. Smoke claws at his throat, nose, and eyes. He chokes back a cough. Rapid footsteps thunder this way and that through the smoke. Snow sprints right across his path, one step crunching his right hand.

After an impossible distance, Snoozy's head thuds against wood. Bear. Would. Bare. Wood. A cabinet. Cabin. Net. Stuck in the cabin net. He's in the kitchen.

He scurries onto the counter. Broken glass digs into his palms. Charred wood sears his palms. Footsteps rush his direction.

He leaps through the smoldering window frame. Bushes slash his face as he crashes to the ground.

A deep breath.

Then another.

And another.

The fresh air stings his split lip, but he doesn't care. He takes another deep—

A heavy weight falls onto his belly. It's Blushful, spilling out the window. Gasping, Snoozy rolls out from under the muscular dwarf. The undaunted Horror wiggles forward, but Snoozy thrusts the fire poker into his eye. Pops the bubble. His former friend twitches once, collapses.

Behind Snoozy, dead leaves crunch. He pivots. The Prince lumbers forward, his head hanging improbably to one side. Struggling to get up, Snoozy yanks the poker out of Blushful's face. Something squishy flies into the air.

Just as the Prince closes in, Snow charges through the window and collides with the undead Horror. They tumble into the bushes with a hiss and a moan.

How the hells is that comb still in her hair?

Before Snoozy can finish taking a grateful breath, Bones scrambles through the kitchen window. Damn. Snoozy hauls himself to his feet and sprints to the backyard. There, clotheslines filled with blankets and mining overalls hang low to the ground like an army of apparitions. Weightless. Snoozy dashes into the clothing, hoping the laundry will distract his pursuers. Waitless.

A breath later, Bones and Snow thrash in the dangling laundry. Snoozy sprints toward his oak tree. Just steps from the tree, he chances a look over his shoulder, but then bumps into something soft and heavy. He turns, bites back a scream. It's the punching bag mounted by Grouchy moons ago. He climbs the tree quickly, knows the branches and handholds as well as he knows his own body.

In the yard, Snow charges through the laundry and halts directly under Snoozy's dangling feet. He holds his breath as Snow and soon Bones stand at the base of the tree, sniffing and hissing at the swaying punching bag. The tree's bark bites into Snoozy's burnt, lacerated palms. It's only a matter of time before the Horrors look up.

Tweeeeet.

A sharp whistle in the distance. A bird?

Snow and Bones hiss in unison, then sprint toward the noise. Toward the mine. Snoozy waits until they are gone, then starts climbing down. His muscles ache, and his trembling palms throb.

Near the ground, a cold hand grips his ankle. Snoozy almost screams. The Prince moans, a terrible noise emanating from somewhere deep inside his rotting gut.

From somewhere empty.

Chapter Sixteen

Grouchy

SHARP TEETH TEAR INTO Grouchy's wounded leg—a precise clamp of pressure on his calf muscle. He spits out dirt and yells, "Run, Merry."

The downed dwarf hears a few of Merry's clumsy steps, then a squeal as Merry spills to the ground. New footsteps crunch over dead leaves, and something heavy drops onto Grouchy's back. A knee.

"I've got a dwarf," says the knee's owner—a deep, human voice. "Hays, call off your dog."

A younger human answers. "You got it, Cap'n. Yanky, c'mere, girl." His voice twangs like a cave-fiddle.

The dog releases Grouchy's leg, but icy fear still grips his belly. His head fumbles with what he's just heard. Human soldiers have captured him, a fate far more terrifying than Snow's curse. She's mindless, but these bastards, they're deliberately evil. When he thinks of destroyed dwarf villages and slaughtered kin, smoldering anger quickly melts his fear.

"On your knees, little one," the captain says, lifting off of him.

The captain's weight rises, and so does Grouchy's anger—like a pot boiling over. Grouchy grits his teeth and rises to his knees, wincing at his throbbing leg.

Tweeeeet.

The captain blows a silver whistle, glowing brilliant by the full moon, and places a spear under Grouchy's chin. He's dressed in a soldier's brown leather armor—deeply worn and accented in ocean blue. A sword hangs at his hip. A metal badge shaped like wings shines on his chest. Under a thick beard, a scar twists his upper lip into a sneer. His eyes are sharper than either his sword or spear. How many dwarfs have fallen before those eyes? How many now rot in pieces?

Steps away, a younger human soldier stands over Merry. Topped with a mop of straw-colored hair, the teen boy holds a sword in one hand and the collar of a massive, drooling dog in the other. Four more soldiers emerge from the forest, none of them old enough to have beards.

Grouchy notices then a number of pale tents pitched beneath the pine trees near the mine's entrance. Nearby, horses pace restlessly and shake their heads. He recognizes the blue banners and crests of the Western Kingdom. This must be the Prince's entourage. *Damn it.* And he has the Prince's fumping sword strapped to his back. Perfect.

"Tattoo, Cracker, scout the path. Monk, Battson, search the prisoners."

The soldiers answer in unison. "Without fail, Captain."

More than a dozen soldiers arrive from camp, some carrying lanterns. The young Hays pulls Merry to his feet. Another soldier with a thin mustache and a sunburnt face pats Merry's bulk.

"Chubby one, ain't ya?" the mustached soldier says, examining the contents of Merry's pockets by lantern light. Merry's eyes go wide. The soldier rummages through the dwarfs' bags, tosses Merry's belongings inside. "He's got a blade, Captain. Not much in the bags except basic supplies. No weapons. A frying pan, some forks. I suppose the forks could be used as a weapon—I know I sure wouldn't want to take a tine to the eyeball, but—"

"That'll do, Monk."

A blond soldier, presumably Battson, puts Grouchy in a headlock. Grouchy tucks his chin to keep the soldier's forearm off his throat. He grunts but says nothing, fights the urge to punch and kick and bite at the filthy swob.

The blond soldier pats—or rather, slaps—Grouchy down and removes the blades, bludgeons, pipe, and tobacco from his pockets. Battson yanks the Prince's sword from his back, then kicks him facedown onto the ground next to Merry. Dead leaves crumble to dust in his beard. He climbs back to his knees.

Battson hands Honey-Stick to the captain. "This little stump had Prince Mikael's sword, Captain. Bloodstained."

Grouchy flinches at the word *stump* and grits his teeth.

"It's the Horrors' blood," Merry says. "They've killed most of us and overrun our cottage, set it ablaze. We're all that's left."

The captain kneels on one knee, eye-to-eye with him and Merry. The Prince's sword rests over his knee. "How did you get this sword? Have you harmed the Prince?" His raspy voice flows rough as salt water over broken seashells.

"It's clear enough, isn't it, Captain?" Battson says. "They lured our Prince here with a tale of a sleeping beauty, then killed and robbed him. I'm just saying. These two are probably scouting our camp so they can murder us, too."

"Stand down, Battson." The captain turns to Grouchy. "I ask again, how did you come in possession of this sword? What are you

---

88 | ROB E. BOLEY

doing out here?"

Grouchy figures he's moments away from execution. He wants to tell this ugly captain to sit on a pike and spin, but he knows it's only a matter of time before the soldiers meet the Horrors. If he can reason with them, he can protect Snow. "Found it in the woods. Near our cottage. Before the Horrors attacked."

"What are these *Horrors*? Are they coming after you?"

He spits. "They're monsters, and yes, they're coming this way. So quit asking me damn questions and prepare your boys, swob."

Battson steps forward, but the captain waves him off. The captain studies Grouchy's eyes as if they were diamonds and he was looking for flaws. Next he turns to Merry, who can't hold his gaze and lowers his eyes. *Dammit, Merry.*

"Is this true?" the captain says. "Did your companion come across our Prince's sword in these woods? Near your cottage? Before the monster attacked?"

"Monsters," Grouchy says, earning a glare from Battson.

"Is it true?" the captain says again.

Merry raises his eyes. "Yes, it's true."

The captain takes three distinct breaths. Grouchy tries to ignore his racing heart and trembling hands. Finally, the captain shakes his head and hands Honey-Stick to Battson.

"They're lying, Battson. Execute them."

Chapter Seventeen

Grouchy

"PLEASE DON'T KILL US." Merry holds up his hands, palms outward. "We'll tell you everything." He smiles sideways at Grouchy. "Won't we, Grouchy?"

"Grouchy, eh?" The captain kneels in front of Merry. "And what's your name? Happy, I suppose?"

"Merry, sir. And you are?"

"Aggravated. Captain Aggravated. *Merry* and *Grouchy*, those don't sound like any dwarf names I've ever heard."

"We received new names when we joined the Collective," Merry says.

By this time, more soldiers have gathered around, many dressed only in bedclothes. All practically boys, they stare down at him and Merry. That's what swobs do. They look down at dwarfs.

The dog whines and stares down the path. Grouchy looks, too, but he sees only twisted shadows and murky moonlight.

"Wouldn't it be easier if we just tortured them?" Battson says. "Just saying."

"Enough, Battson." The captain alternates his gaze between him and Merry. "You dwarfs live here, on human land?"

Merry nods. "We were outcasts in our own villages. Bones, our leader, brought us together to form the Collective. We—"

"Shut your shithole, Merry," Grouchy says.

The captain shoots him a hard stare. Still holding Grouchy's eyes, he says, "No, Merry. Continue."

"We work in the mine, gathering gemstones. Otherwise, we live off the land—"

"You poach gems from King Francis? You're brave dwarfs, I'll give you that."

Merry shakes his head. "No, Bones had an arrangement with King Francis. We paid a rent of valuable gems. In exchange, we were left alone."

"Where is this Bones? Can you take me to him?"

"He's become one of the monsters."

"Of course he has."

"If we're done with bedtime stories," Battson says, "I'll gladly beat the truth out of these little stumps."

"Battson, go away."

"But, Captain, I—"

"Now, Battson."

Muttering, Battson trudges a respectful distance away, though still within earshot. Grouchy shoots him a dirty look and spits on the ground. The dog whines more urgently, tugging against its leash.

"Hays, control your animal."

"I'm sorry, Cap'n. She's shaking like a pig passing a poker."

In unison, the horses whine and buck. *Balls. Something sinister this way comes.*

The captain considers the dwarfs. "Tell me, Merry. What happened to the Prince? Is he okay?"

Merry looks at the human, then at Grouchy. "He's a monster, too."

"And how did that happen? How did the Prince become a monster?"

"He was bitten."

Grouchy can't take it anymore. "Balls. The Prince kissed our lady Snow. She woke up cursed. Rabid. She bit the Prince and Bones. The curse spread to them. They attacked us. And I stabbed your precious Prince through the heart."

"You murderous little shitpile," Battson says. "Do you know the punishment for killing a noble?"

"He ain't dead," Grouchy says.

"You stabbed him through the heart." The captain speaks very slowly. "But he's not dead?"

"He still walks. Seen it myself."

"Don't tell me you believe this fairy tale, Captain?" Battson fidgets with Honey-Stick's handle.

At that moment, the dog breaks free, running into the woods away from the scream.

"Yanky," Hays yells, too late.

Across camp, wood snaps and hooves pound. The horses stampede through the woods.

"Gather up, Blumers," the captain yells. "We're heading down the path. On foot, apparently."

The young soldiers shout in unison. "Without fail, Captain."

"What about them?" Battson says, nudging Grouchy's ass with his boot.

"Leave them with the Page. He might as well make himself useful."

Battson yanks Grouchy to his feet and clamps shackles over his wrists. The metal bites down hard enough that Grouchy's fingers go numb. The soldiers grab the dwarfs' bags, and Battson shoves him toward the tents.

In the camp, soldiers run in all directions, retrieving swords and spears, lighting lanterns, and sliding into boots and armor. Once out of the captain's sight, Battson kicks Grouchy hard in the ass. He offers no response, but anger boils in his belly.

"Should we take their beards?" Hays asks Battson.

Battson and Merry respond simultaneously.

"My what?"

"Their what?"

"Their beards," Hays repeats. "Dwarfs melt gold and silver into thin strands and wear it as beards. That's why they're so short, right? Because they're weighed down by all that metal?"

"Fumping hells," Grouchy says.

Merry smiles at the young soldier. "You've been misinformed."

"Dammit, Randa," Hays says under his breath. "So, uh, what are these monsters like?"

"Vicious and savage," Merry says. "They want only to bite and kill. They cannot be reasoned with. They—"

"Enough," Battson says. "These little shits are murderous liars, pinky. Don't let them pollute your virgin ears."

They soon reach a canvas tent with a pointy top. It stands adjacent to the largest tent in the camp—clearly the Prince's. The soldiers drop the dwarfs' bags outside the tent. Battson doesn't bother knocking, simply shoves Grouchy through the doorway. His busted, bitten leg fails him, and he sprawls onto the floor.

A skinny man sits up in bed, eyes wide as the moon. He's a bit older than the soldiers, but skinny, with a neck like a goose and short, spiky hair. He reminds Grouchy of a marionette puppet. His tent is a cluttered mess of clothing, documents, sewing gear, various brushes, and an assortment of creams and lotions. It reeks of incense and spices.

"What's happening?" the foppish man says. "I heard a whistle."

Battson yanks Grouchy to his knees. "The camp is under siege by dwarfs, Page. No telling how bad it will get. We have taken two stump prisoners. You must watch them."

"Me?"

"Yes, you."

"Why me?"

Battson puffs out his chest, the arrogant ass. "Because the real men must search the woods for the rest of these murderous runts."

"Murderous?" the Page says, looking at him and Merry. "Where is my Prince?"

Battson kicks Grouchy's gut, and the air leaps abruptly out of his lungs. He doubles over, gasping for air. But the soldier pulls him back upright by the hair.

"This one stabbed the Prince through the heart." Battson offers the Prince's sword handle-first to the Page. As the Page takes the sword, Battson whispers loud enough for all to hear. "He had the Prince's sword when we captured him. Blood-stained. Do what you will. I'm just saying. No court would bring charges against you."

Battson bends over Grouchy and releases his hair. Grouchy suspects a verbal taunt is coming, so he jerks his head backward and slams it into the human's face.

"Ow," Battson yells, then kicks the back of his head.

Grouchy's ears ring and a bomb ignites in his skull. He lands on his chin, and fireflies whirl lazily in his vision. Hells, it was worth it. When he struggles back to his knees, he and Merry are now alone with the Page. He breathes, winces, and breathes again. If he ever sees that Battson again, that swob will be sorry.

"You stabbed . . . my Prince?" The Page speaks to the dwarfs, but stares only at the sword in his trembling hands.

Merry clears his throat. "The Prince was overcome with a terrible curse. Grouchy stabbed him in self-defense."

The Page's lower lip trembles. A tear drips down his sculpted cheek. He points the blade at Grouchy and speaks through clenched teeth.

"You killed my Prince."

Chapter Eighteen

Battson

ONCE OUTSIDE THE PAGE'S tent, Battson leads Hays through camp. He rubs his chin, bruised by that nasty stump's big head. His blood thumps in his veins. Finally, he and his fellow grunts—the Blumers—are going to see some real action. All the better that it involves stumps.

"Why so heavy back there?" says Hays, the dumb hick. "We don't know what the dwarfs did."

Battson's tempted to punch Hays in the face, to finish what was started at that dingy bar in Hays' shit-house town. Instead, he grabs Hays' shoulders.

"They're guilty of being filthy stumps, pinky. They deserve whatever punishment they receive."

Hays stares back at him. Until this idiot's recruitment, Battson was the Blumers' pinky, or newest recruit. The other soldiers are always hard on the pinky, which is all part of earning respect. They sure as hell were hard on Battson, but most of the grunts have already warmed to Hays. And Captain seems unusually fond of him, which only irritates Battson all the more.

He leads Hays into the woods, tries to ignore the deep holes of shadow. Behind every tree, he imagines the bane of his childhood bedtime, Rip the Tearer, lurking, waiting to strike. Rip only killed here in the Eastern Kingdom, but even as a child in the Western Kingdom the murderer's deeds haunted Battson's dreams. Even now, he pictures hateful eyes watching him, a jagged blade twitching to rend his flesh, and a crooked smile eager to mock his suffering.

They soon catch up with the Blue Meridian platoon. The path is lit only by lanterns and moonlight. He walks beside Captain. Steps ahead, Smiley and Monk take point. The rest of the grunts are paired off behind them.

Battson stares into the flickering shadows. "Little spuds probably have booby-traps."

Captain says, "Uh-huh."

"Probably trained the squirrels to attack us."

"You ever see what a squirrel can do to a man?" Monk whispers. "I had a cousin once . . ." He continues ranting about shadows and dwarfs and rabid squirrels, but Battson tunes him out. Mostly. ". . .their chatter. No animal alive can curse like a squirrel . . ." Above, the moon weaves in and out of the clouds, casts a slowly strobing light. ". . . I once met a guy who passed out with a bag of nuts in his—"

"Monk, shut your meathole." Captain stops, holds up his hand. "Everyone shut up." He stands there, eyes closed, head cocked. Finally, Captain says, "I hate this forest. I miss the ocean at night and the salty morning air. Here in the East, there's no waves—just crickets and hairy things scampering in the trees. Bats fluttering overhead. Snakes wiggling under the tents. But listen. Do any of you hear any of those things now?"

Captain's right. The silent forest makes Battson think of the stories they heard in the nearby lumberjack shithole Abundance— stories of bones found near the river stripped clean of flesh yet bearing no teeth marks. The locals had hired a hunter—a giant of a man—to slay this beast. He thought it superstition at the time, but now he's not so sure.

The Blumers left Abundance and found the mine yesternight. Of course, no road led here. It was Tattoo and Hays' dog Yanky who tracked the mine. After camping for the night, the Prince insisted that he visit the cottage alone come morning. After the Prince left, Captain spent the day running his grunts through training drills. By nightfall, still no Prince.

"Do you think the Prince is really dead?" Battson says.

Captain shrugs. "At this point, I almost don't care. Go. Know. Bow. Row. Foe. Bestow. Glow. Doe. Toe. You know what these words have in common, son?"

Battson sighs. "Yeah, Captain. They all rhyme with Snow."

The soldiers within earshot chuckle.

Captain nods. "Yeah. They sure do."

The love songs. The worst part about this mission with the Prince has definitely been the love songs. Back when they first left the Western Kingdom, the Blumers were under the mistaken impression that theirs was an urgent diplomatic mission related to Queen Adara's rumored disappearance. Or perhaps related to the approaching winter—because the Prince kept speaking to his foppish Page about snow, snow, snow. While the Prince met with King Francis in Platessa, the soldiers learned from a chef at the Chamber House that Snow was a girl who worked in the kitchen. The Prince had been sending her love letters since spring until she disappeared. Of course, the Prince's love for Snow didn't keep him from trying to bed every maiden in the Eastern Kingdom, but it did prompt him to compose—and perform—a number of love songs.

Smiley looks back at Battson and laughs, his breath strong with drink. "You see Tattoo's new ink?"

Before the dwarfs arrived, Battson, Smiley, and Monk had been playing a game of Goldeneye. Battson had flipped a golden coin into Smiley's mug, and Smiley had dutifully drunk it all down—including the coin.

Battson shakes his head.

Smiley grins. "It's the Prince. Well, it's him from the waist up, but it's a cross between a jackrabbit and a jackass below. I won't explain the beast's privates—"

"Thank you for that."

"But he's being ridden like a horse by—"

Someone screams down the path—a horrible noise punctuated by a gargled choke. The Blumers immediately take defensive positions, swords and spears at the ready.

Ahead, rapid footsteps approach. The full moon peeks from behind a cloud, its pale light illuminating the path. Battson squeezes the handle of his sword, imagines the metal thirsting for dwarf blood.

Whatever's coming, it's fast.

Captain holds up a hand. "Easy, grunts. It's Tattoo."

Battson squints. Tattoo sprints toward them, panting. His leather chest armor is torn, exposing his tattoos and something else. Blood? Looks as if the ink frozen under Tattoo's skin has come alive: wet and dripping.

"Monk," Captain says. "You have the medic kit?"

"Yeah, Captain." Monk waves to Tattoo. "Tattoo, you alright?"

No. He's not.

Tattoo hisses and tackles Monk at full speed. Monk thuds to the ground. Smiley grabs Tattoo's shoulder.

"Smiley, watch—" Battson's words come too late.

Tattoo lunges at Smiley's face as if to kiss him. He hears flesh being torn from bone. Smiley convulses.

"Hold Tattoo," Captain shouts.

Tattoo charges Captain, but Battson kicks the rabid grunt to the ground. Even through Battson's boot, Tattoo's body radiates feverish heat. Two more grunts grapple with Tattoo but quickly curse, shout, then hiss.

Battson hears footsteps behind him, turns just in time to see Cracker charging. They collapse in a tangle. Cracker shoves his face at Battson's neck, but the soldier keeps his hands around Cracker's throat. Where Cracker's nose should be is now a torn hole dripping blood. It spurts onto his hands, hot and sticky. They've wrestled before, but Cracker's never been this strong. Cracker gnashes his teeth, spitting blood and drool into the air. Battson struggles, but loses traction.

He closes his eyes, waits for the bite.

Chapter Nineteen

Captain Ritchards

CAPTAIN RITCHARDS SEES CRACKER take Battson down, and he hopes that the young soldier will take care of himself. Of course, he doesn't.

Ritchards sidesteps a flailing grunt and plunges his sword into Cracker's chest. The blade shakes as Cracker convulses, gurgles, and goes limp. His own grunt, one of his own. *Damn it.* He kicks the corpse aside and offers a hand.

"On your feet, grunt. We've got monsters to kill."

All around them, soldiers shout, fight, hiss, curse, and bite. The darkness makes it impossible to tell friend from foe. Glass shatters as someone steps on a fallen lantern. Flames sprout and gobble at dead leaves and bushes.

Something grabs his boot. He looks down, just as Cracker—somehow still moving—bites into his boot. He grunts at the pressure of the bite, kicks free with his other leg.

He steps away, tries to process what his senses just told him. He stabbed Cracker through the heart. Cracker's eyes were glazed.

He was dead, but somehow not. Ritchards blows his whistle, but the Blumers are in chaos.

Tweeeeet.

"—that Shrub? I couldn't tell if—"

"—okay, Jellyfish. Let me—ow, the spud bit m—"

"—the hell off of me—"

Grunts run in all directions. The scents of smoke, blood, urine, and burning leaves assault his nostrils. His boys jostle together. Chewie chases Teddy-Bear into the forest. A soldier knocks Hen to the ground. Hen screams and then hisses. Nearby, Antler screams, and Hays turns to assist. Except the grunt Jellyfish is already huddled over Antler, apparently helping. Antler screams. Jellyfish bites into Antler's wrist. Bones crunch, yet Antler doesn't scream. No, he hisses. Hays pukes, hot bile projecting onto the ground.

Ritchards grabs Hays and pulls him back. Jellyfish and Antler lunge, but Ritchards stabs Antler in the chest. Battson slices Jellyfish's throat.

"Brilliant time to join the Service, pinky," Battson says.

"To the mine," Ritchards yells. "Now."

Battson, Hays, and Monk sprint back down the path, and Ritchards scans the crowd for any other survivors. He has no choice but to retreat. He's lost grunts before from not knowing when it was time to pull out. He won't make that mistake again.

He puts the whistle to his lips. Normally, it tastes like cold, hard truth. Right now, it tastes like fear.

Tweeeeet.

"Retreat to the mine."

He turns, follows his soldiers to the mine. His lungs feel like worn rags in this thin mountain air. Behind, dozens of footsteps drum the earth—no telling how many are friend or foe. More screams stab the quiet night.

Ahead, the ghostly tents of camp. Almost there.

Behind, pounding footsteps close in. Abruptly, a choking scream replaces those steps. He doesn't know which of his fellow grunts falls. If the soldier had been a little faster, the monsters would've grabbed Ritchards instead.

Finally, he reaches the mine. Across the entrance spans a metal gate—thick metal held closed with a built-in lock—smiling wickedly at them like a toothy grin. Monk tugs the gate, but it won't budge.

Ritchards smacks the metal. "Damn."

Battson wiggles his dagger into the lock. Metal scrapes against metal, but to no avail. Ritchards nudges him aside and thrusts his own sword into the lock, wrenching his blade left and right. The lock clicks open. When he removes his sword, the tip is split like a forked tongue.

Behind them, sprinting footsteps approach.

Battson turns and swings his sword. The runner ducks and slides feet first into the gate with a loud clang. If the monsters didn't know where the soldiers had fled, they know now for sure.

"Dammit," the runner says, "it's me, Shrub."

Ritchards yanks Shrub—so named because of his copious body hair—to his feet, and Hays pulls open the gate. Ritchards pushes his grunts through the gate, but a strong hand grabs him by the neck and yanks him backward. He trips, falls on his ass. Standing over him is a soldier—its face rendered unrecognizable by bites. Blood drips hot onto Ritchards' face. With a hiss, the monster reaches down for him, but Hays spins the soldier around, kicks it on its back, and stabs his sword through its stomach and into the ground. It gasps a choking gurgle and then collapses.

After Hays pulls him to his feet, Ritchards pats his pinky on the back, pulls him into the mine, and slams the gate. "C'mon. These monsters don't stay dead."

As if to prove his point, the faceless soldier's hands twitch. It struggles to sit up, its torso sliding up and down Hays' blade. The sword saws against the monster's ribs and makes wet clicking noises, like a stuttering cricket. Propped up on its elbows, the thing stares at them and moans.

"That ain't natural," Hays says.

Battson shrugs.

Shrub and Monk curse.

Ritchards shakes his head slowly.

"I think that's Bruiser," Shrub says.

Ritchards sighs. "Not anymore it isn't."

A gold coin plops out of the soldier's guts.

"No," Battson says, "it's Smiley."

Down the path, a few straggling grunts scream and plead for what seems an eternity. His grunts. His boys. The cacophony ceases abruptly. Smiley moans. Leaves scatter. A solitary hiss pierces the dark, and then a chorus of hisses and footsteps swarms toward the mine.

Chapter Twenty

Prince Mikael

EVER FORWARD.
 Hunger.
Bellyache.
 So cold.
One long shiver.
 Mouth to heel.
Neck stiff.
 Fingers pop.
Trees. Shadows. Full moon. Meat runs down trail. Into darkness.
Meat sweats and pants. Meat sees not.
 Reach out.
 Grab meat.
Bite neck.
 Flesh warm.
Swallow.
 Bite again.
For one moment, cold fades. Death fades. Alive. Another bite. So

alive. Skin and muscle. Warm.
Another bite.
Meat cools.
Useless.
Lifeless.
Ever forward.
Hunger.

Chapter Twenty-One

Grouchy

"MERCY," GROUCHY SAYS. "PLEASE have mercy. Just kill me."

But the Page shows no mercy. Instead he prattles on, his eyes lost in an imagined distance. "My first memory is of my Prince. Only four years old, I was in Seaside Castle for the very first time, a brilliantly shiny palace full of vibrant colors, plush furnishings, and massive fish tanks filled with wondrous creatures. My father held my hand as we entered the royal nursery. My Prince, just a baby, was wailing. I asked my father why my Prince was mad."

"Most nobles are," Grouchy says.

In the distance, soldiers yell and scream and—quickly becoming Horrors themselves—hiss. Grouchy can't even enjoy the sound of dying swobs, because it means that Snow now has an army.

"'He's just a baby,' said Father. My Prince's nursemaid knelt and kissed my cheeks. She put my palm over my Prince's head, already covered in dark wisps of hair. She introduced us and told him I'd be his best friend and most loyal servant. And you know what? He stopped crying." Here, the Page bursts into tears. He stares down at Honey-Stick. "I remember when he received this sword. Such a work of art, not unlike my Prince himself. His initials are engraved on the handle. M.A.M., for Mikael Algore McNimby. But to me, he was simply 'my Prince.'"

"I'm sure he was a wonderful individual," Merry says, smile trembling above his chins.

"Balls, we haven't time for this. Snow. Let us go. Time is short."

"Time?" the Page says. "What matters now the passing of time?"

"What about the passing of you, you prick? You'll die here."

"My life is worthless now."

The Page places the blade's tip to his chest and swallows. He takes a deep breath, braces himself.

"There's better ways to off yourself," Grouchy says. "Cut your wrists lengthwise. It's assloads easier. More reliable, too. But for fump's sake, unshackle us first. We don't—"

A horrifying scream—much too close—cuts off Grouchy's words, followed immediately by a terrible hiss. The losing battle is now in the camp. Yelling. Hissing.

"Your soldiers are dying," Merry says.

"No," Grouchy says. "They're becoming monsters. Horrors. So will we. Just like your Prince."

"My Prince? If he has become a monster, then so shall I. I'll follow my Prince to hell, if needed."

Outside, a twig snaps. The Page drops the sword and gasps. Grouchy tries climbing to his feet. Maybe if he tackles the Horror he can overpower it somehow, use his shackles as a weapon.

The tent flap opens.

There, Snoozy stares wearily at them with his bruised face and split lip. He holds a blood-stained fire poker.

"Snoozy," Merry says. "You're alive."

"And I'm not dead, either."

Snoozy takes the Prince's sword from the Page, who gasps again, then slams the blade through their shackles. Sparks fly. Metal snaps. A breeze through the open flap blows out all of the Page's candles. Grouchy shivers.

He pats Snoozy's belly, takes the sword. "Good to see you."

"It is, isn't it?"

Then Grouchy notices that Snoozy's jaws are chewing something. He narrows his eyes, but Snoozy shakes his head and opens his mouth wide.

"It's only the Prince's honey-gum," Snoozy says. "Let's go."

Outside, Horrors chase down the remaining soldiers like wild dogs. Grouchy runs onward, ignores the stabbing pain in his leg. When the dwarfs reach the mine, a sword pins an undead soldier to the ground outside the entrance. The Horror squirms and moans.

Five soldiers stand behind the gate. Swobs. In his mine. And of course, one of them is that ass-pit Battson.

"Let us in," Grouchy says. "We haven't much time."

"Why should we?" Battson says. "This is all your fault. I'm just saying."

"Like hells it is. Your dandy-ass Prince started this by kissing on our Snow. These woods were fine 'til you swob idiots showed up."

"Let them in, Battson," the captain says wearily. "They know these monsters better than us, and they sure as hell know this mine better."

"But Captain—"

"Now."

Battson kicks open the gate, and Merry steps inside.

Grouchy follows, pauses to examine the lock. "You broke the lock? Brilliant."

"We couldn't get in," Hays says.

"What's wrong with your friend?" The captain nods toward the gate.

Outside, Snoozy stares at the undead soldier pinned to the earth, still sluggishly snapping its jaw. The addled dwarf steps on the Horror's throat.

"Snooze," Grouchy says. "What are you fumping doing?"

Snoozy wrestles with the blade embedded in the Horror's chest. He twists it free with a wet slopping noise and shoves it downward through the Horror's temple. The Horror twitches once, then rests. Still as a fallen tree.

"That's how you get to the clapping," Snoozy says. "Pop the bubble."

Grouchy grabs the addled dwarf. "Well done, Snooze. Handy tip. Now please get your crazy ass in here."

Quick footsteps approach. Pivoting, Grouchy raises Honey-Stick, ready to take down whatever's coming. It's just the Page, still dressed only in pajama bottoms, his wide eyes stained pink from crying. Grouchy knows that look all too well—heartbreak.

"They're coming," the Page says. "So many."

Grouchy shoves everyone inside and slams the gate shut with a hollow clang that reverberates through the tunnels.

Ahead is the mine's staging chamber, a wide space used mostly for storing gear, sorting gemstones, enjoying several mid-day meals, and repairing tools. A cramped tunnel—about a dozen or so dwarf paces long—separates the staging chamber from the gate.

His braided beard covered in blood and ash, Snoozy drops the gory sword and sits down in the tunnel. A soldier retrieves the blade, wipes it on a gem bag.

Grouchy kneels in front of the gate. "These ass-pits broke the lock."

"Wonderful," Snoozy says. He pulls out a rope. "Let's put a bow on the present before it becomes the past."

Merry grabs the rope and addresses the captain. "These Horrors aren't burdened with great intelligence. It'll take them awhile to figure out that the gate can only be pulled open. Hopefully enough time to seal the tunnel."

Grouchy frowns. "That's a fumpload of hope."

Something slams into the gate behind Grouchy. A rough hand grabs his hair and yanks his head back into the bars. Sprinkles flutter in his vision, otherwise dark. His skull throbs. Hot breath flushes against his neck. He doesn't feel the bite, but blood blossoms wet and hot over his

Chapter Twenty-Two

Grouchy

GROUCHY EXPECTS A HISS to erupt from his mouth, but instead a string of obscenities comes out.

"Jumping shit cakes alive. Fumping hells."

The blood pouring over his neck is not his own. It belongs to the Horror, which now has the captain's sword embedded in its face. As Grouchy stumbles forward, the Horror collapses against the gate, trampled underfoot by another cursed soldier.

Then another. And another. And still more.

In seconds, cursed soldiers in various stages of disrepair mash against the gate. One of the soldiers has a bare chest covered in blood, gore, and tattoos. Behind Grouchy, swob soldiers stand in his mine. In front of him, a whole mob of cursed swobs wait, eager for his flesh. And he's stuck in the middle. He's had many nightmares involving swobs, his father, or usually some combination, but nothing this horrifying. Could the night get any worse?

At the mob's rear, he glimpses his Snowflake. Her eyes—blood-red and coal-black—gape wide with ravenous hunger. Her once-pouty lips sneer across her perfect teeth. How in the hells is that comb still in her hair?

The mob surges against the gate, smashing those at the front against the metal. Those at the back scramble forward, saliva and blood dripping from their mouths. The gate whines.

"How strong is that gate?" the captain says. "Will it hold?"

"It was designed to stop bears," Merry says, "but bears aren't quite that, um, exuberant."

"Or plentiful," Snoozy adds. "Or dancing or wooden."

"It won't hold," Grouchy says.

The captain sheathes a forked blade. "What can we do?"

"Seal the entrance." Grouchy takes a breath and steels himself for what comes next. "Merry, thoughts?"

Merry stares back at Grouchy in surprise, then points at the Page. "You, light all of these lanterns and put them at the rear of this staging chamber. Grouchy and Snoozy, gather as many of the busted pickaxes as you can. You soldiers, we need you working at these support beams." He points to the thick lengths of wood supporting the tunnel between the gate and the staging chamber.

Battson shakes his ugly head. "No way. I'm just saying. We take the support beams and the roof will cave in over us. Leaving you dwarfs safe in your mine. Forget it."

"No time for this, damn it." Grouchy hurls a box of matches to the Page. The sad little prick's ankle is bleeding. He files that detail away. "Do as you're told."

Battson snorts. "Since when do we take—"

"Enough, Battson," the captain says. "My grunts will work the support beams."

Grouchy and Snoozy cobble together some decent pickaxes, all with chipped blades and cracked handles. Grouchy leaves Honey-Stick in the staging area, then runs to the entrance tunnel. There, the swobs hack at the beams with their swords, covering the ground with splintered wood.

Grouchy's knee throbs. His dog-bitten calf flexes and bleeds. Damn that bitch. He tosses a pickaxe to the captain. "Hit the ceilings and walls. Destabilize the opening." It feels good to bark orders at a swob.

He slams his own pickaxe into the wall, and the impact ripples to his spine. Sparks flash, and a fist-sized chunk of rock falls to the ground. Soon everyone—human and dwarf—pounds at the walls.

Dust and sparks pepper the air. He and the captain work closest to the gate. The racket of metal striking rock obscures almost all other noise—except for the gate rattling on its hinges. He steals a glance. The Horrors fling themselves at the metal as carelessly as one might dive into deep water. The gate won't last much longer.

He slams his pickaxe into the wall, and the handle shatters. The pick arcs backward, where someone yells in pain. At that moment, the rock above lurches.

In the periphery of his vision there's a blur of motion by the gate.

Metal clicks loudly.

Grouchy yanks the captain backward, but they stumble over debris. The mountain clears its throat, and the surrounding tunnel collapses. Massive chunks of rock collide, crash, and collapse.

Grouchy's buried alive.

Rubble smothers his limbs. Rock dust fills his mouth. Before the darkness settles behind his eyes, he has time to ask himself that age-old question.

————— ◆ —————

"SO, THAT IS HOW it ends?" Snow asked him.

They were sitting in the forest, where moments prior Snow had found Grouchy lying flat on his back on the ground. Not familiar with dwarfen prayer, she'd thought him injured. She'd knelt and jostled him out of his meditations. When he'd opened his eyes, he saw her bosom dangling inside the neckline of her dress.

His prayers had been answered.

This prompted a discussion on dwarf rituals and beliefs.

Snow continued summarizing his words. "Your soul is a teardrop-shaped cloud in your stomach, and when you die, your soul pours out through your eye sockets and mouth and forms three invisible clouds, which eventually rain upon the Earth, soak into the soil, and rejoin the great OverSoul burning at the Earth's core? You're shitting me. Dwarf heaven is a big fire cave?"

"More or less."

"Your heaven is our hell," Snow said. "Don't the flames hurt?"

"Not without flesh," Grouchy said. "The soul's like water. Can't be burned. It leaves the body as a cloud and hovers among loved ones. Eventually, the soul says its goodbyes. Then it rains into the Earth and is boiled into steam."

"What about us humans? Is there a place for us in your heaven?"

Grouchy rubbed his temples. "Most dwarfs would say no."

"Do you dwarfs have any theories about where we come from? The three arks, I mean. Adults only offer the murkiest of explanations. When we're young, we talk about it all the time. But something happens to us when we become older. We stop caring about where we're from. It'll happen to me soon. What think you?"

"Most of us think you came from the stars—the hellish white holes in the night sky."

Snow nodded. "If heaven is below earth, then your hells must be above."

Several generations ago, the dwarfs were the sole inhabitants of the Land. The ancient tribes lived in the Land's middle region—a hilly land with deep, meandering cave systems. When the first humans arrived on the western coast aboard two massive arks, they had been at sea for years, and none of them could agree for how long or from where they came. The humans had been looking for land for so long that it had become an almost mythical concept. So, when their long journey finally ended, they dubbed their new home simply "Land." In those early years, the dwarfs co-existed peacefully with the humans, who settled on the Land's western and eastern sides. The Western Kingdom was the oldest human settlement, a land of ocean coasts, beaches, and hills—very different from the massive trees, deep forests, and magnificent mountains here in the Eastern Kingdom.

Snow paused, bit her lip. "But why is your soul just split three ways? Why not five, if it came out the nostrils? Or seven, if the ears?"

"Three is our sacred number. Represents our ancestors, ourselves, and our offspring. Past, present, and future."

"Offspring. Hmmm." Snow patted Grouchy's leg. "Think you'll ever have any of your own? Surely a dwarf as handsome as you will take a wife?"

His cheeks burned. Sweat dampened his armpits. He shrugged. "So, what happens after death for humans?"

Snow shrugged. "The Hopefuls say that if you believe in the Ascension, your soul will be allowed into the Betweenplace. From there, you'll work and toil to make up for all the sins you've committed on the World Below. And when you're done with that, you'll toil some more to make up for your ancestors' sins. And when your debt is paid, you just float there, waiting for the Ascension and the rise to Heaven."

Decades after the arks arrived, the third ark, the Moncansas, arrived. This ark was full of deeply religious humans known as the Hopefuls. Their doctrine saw the dwarfs as a lesser species to be not only controlled but eradicated. The Hopefuls started the Purge and established the Ascendio Kingdom on the dwarfs' land.

"What if you don't believe in the Ascension?" he said.

"Then you're stuck in the World Below—hell—a terrible burden to any family members who follow you in death. You writhe in constant agony until the Ascension cleanses you to nothingness."

"That's what all humans believe?"

Snow shook her head, and he caught a whiff of her scent— flowers, fruit, and cream. "That's just the Hopefuls. Most folks are just Hopish. They believe in Heaven, but not all the Hopeful's rules. And they only believe in the Ascension because they're scared not to."

"What do you believe?"

"Shit, I never had much use for heaven."

He grinned. "Everyone needs something to believe in. Something better than this." He waved his hand at the world around them. "Otherwise, we'd all go mad by the sad desperation of it all."

She tilted her head, licked her lips. "You know what I really believe happens?"

"Go on."

"You rot. Your flesh becomes meat and fertilizer." She scooped up a handful of dirt. "You feed hungry plants or hungrier animals. You become dirt and shit. You give back a bit of what you've taken, and hopefully everyone has a nice meal."

A mosquito landed on her cheek, and he brushed it away. His belly churned at the brief contact.

"A bit gruesome, yeah?"

"No." Snow spilled the dirt. "I think it's beautiful."

———— ◆ ————

AND SHE WAS RIGHT.

It is beautiful.

He enjoys peace, but only for a moment.

Hands clamp onto his shoulders and drag him free of the rocks. Wood splinters jut into his neck and arms. It's Hays who pulls him out of the rubble and into the staging chamber. Without another word, the soldier returns to the rubble, where the other soldiers are digging.

Grouchy holds up a bruised hand with a couple broken fingers—throbbing as if each contained a miniature heart. A thin line of blood slides down his temple into his dusty beard. He pulls off his left boot, winces. His big toe's purple, probably broken. He shakes his head and inhales the mine's familiar scent of dust and mineral. Smells like the truth. Cold truth. His clothes—still stinking of smoke—hang heavy with sweat. His skin prickles with chilled goose bumps.

He watches the soldiers pull the captain out of the rubble and prop him up.

"You alright, Cap'n?" Hays says.

He coughs, shakes his head. "Hell. A mountain fell on me." Coughs. "Do I look alright? Where's Grouchy?" Cough. "He pulled me back just in time."

"Over here," Grouchy says.

"Thanks, Grouchy."

He saved a swob's life. Not just any swob, but a soldier. A captain. If the captain survives this night, how many dwarfs will he kill and maim in the years ahead? Still, the swob did save his life. He spits blood. "We're even."

"I wasn't keeping score."

"Good thing." Merry wipes his face. "Because no one's winning here."

"The present hasn't yet passed," Snoozy says, bandaging a gash in his shoulder.

"Well, it will soon," Merry says. "Listen."

Everyone stops for a moment.

Tchk. Tchk. Tchk.

The dwarfs hear it first—rocks scrambling. The mob is already digging at the cave-in from the other side. Relentlessly.

Endlessly.

"Listen for what?" Battson says.

"They're digging through," Grouchy says.

The captain wipes his brow with a trembling hand. "Is there another way out of here?"

Grouchy chuckles. "We caved in the only exit."

Chapter Twenty-Three

Captain Ritchards

CAPTAIN RITCHARDS INVENTORIES HIS grunts. Battson is scraped and bruised, but otherwise fine. A cut on Shrub's forehead streams blood. Monk is relatively unscathed—too much to hope that a falling rock would break his jaw and silence his constant yammering. Hays' right ear is bleeding. This is all that's left of the Blue Meridian platoon.

He shivers, surprised by the mine's cooler temperature. He and his grunts sit on the cave-in rubble. The dwarfs sit on the staging area floor, where the Page rocks slowly back and forth on top of a locker.

"So, we're stuck here?" Battson says. "I'm just saying. Great plan, stumps."

Ritchards smacks Battson's shoulder. "Not helping. It'll take them hours to dig through the tunnel. Plenty of time to organize a stand against them."

"Agreed," Grouchy says. "But first, let's make sure no Horrors are in here with us."

Ritchards bites back a smile at the bearded dwarf's high-pitched voice. "What do you mean?"

Tchk. Tchk. Tchk.

Grouchy points at the Page. "That gash on your ankle. Were you bit?"

Cobb blinks his teary eyes. "I don't know. One of those things came into my tent after you left. I threw a mirror and a trunk of clothes at it. The tent collapsed, and I crawled out. There were shards of mirror everywhere."

Ritchards stands, and stars spiral in the periphery of his vision. What the hell is wrong with him? "If he was bit, he'd be one of those monsters now, right?"

"We call them Horrors." Merry offers a crooked smile. "The undead ones, we've been calling the cold Horrors. If they bite you, it takes hours for the curse to overtake you. That's what happened to Blushful."

"Explain," Ritchards says, a ball of ice churning in his stomach.

"He was just weak at first," Merry says. "His wound didn't hurt, but was numb, tingling. Soon his body slowed down. He grew cold and tired, pale." Merry smacks his hands together. "Then he turned into one of those hissing maniacs. We call them the hot Horrors."

No. Dammit, no.

"We tried giving him raylee root," says Snoozy, the new dwarf who's staring hard at Merry. "But the patient was so impatient."

The dwarf's inflection and Merry's darting eyes tell him that something's amiss between these dwarfs. Something about this raylee root?

Tchk. Tchk. Tchk.

Ritchards eyes Cobb's wound. "Does your wound hurt? Does it tingle?"

"No. Yes. I mean, it hurts quite a lot. It doesn't tingle."

Monk wipes the wound with a dirty rag. "Doesn't look like a bite to me, Captain. And I know a thing or two about bites. My girl once had this pet rabbit that would—"

"Then let's not worry about it," Ritchards says. He loses his legs and hides it by falling backward onto the rubble.

Tchk. Tchk. Tchk.

"The digging is getting louder," Grouchy says.

Merry nods. "Closer."

"Any weapons in here?" Monk rummages through a trunk. "If we're going to be taking on that entire horde, we need more weapons. Oh! Do you have arrows? What am I talking about? Why would you?" He squats next to Grouchy. "Don't probably fire a lot of arrows in the mining business, do you? But I'm wagering you have some more shovels?"

Grouchy grunts. "There's another option."

Ritchards blinks hard through wobbling vision. His heart flutters. "Go on."

"We trap them in the northwest passage. There's a doctor in the town downriver, in Abundance."

"Dr. Killington? He told the Prince about your Snow."

Grouchy frowns at that. "We think he can cure them."

Tchk. Tchk. Tchk.

Battson waves his hands, casting flickering shadows over his battered face. "Why the hell would we capture these things? I'm just saying. We kill them. End of problem."

Monk clears his throat. "The Horrors will be bottlenecked as they come through the cave-in. We can take them down one at a time."

"Some of those *Horrors* are our friends," Grouchy says, between clenched teeth.

"And the rest are *our* friends." Battson points at the cave-in.

"So don't think—"

"No, Battson," Ritchards says. "The rest are *my grunts*. I'll decide what's best for them. Besides, what do you think our Queen Theabella would say if we came home without her Prince? If we didn't try everything in our power to cure her son?"

Battson lowers his head. Ritchards knows he's a smart kid and a hell of a fighter, but he's undisciplined. And he's got a boulder on his back as big a whale. So much anger. Not unlike this dwarf Grouchy.

He motions toward the dwarf. "Continue."

"You ever been in a mine?"

He shakes his head.

Tchk. Tchk. Tchk.

Grouchy grabs a fist-sized diamond from a split bag on the floor and scratches onto the wall a diagram of the northwest passage. While Grouchy is drawing, introductions are made. Monk helps Merry with Snoozy's lacerated shoulder. The dwarfs all have worn eyes and numb faces.

Numb. Damn it.

It all happened so fast, back on the trail. Ritchards fingers the tear in his boot where, earlier, Cracker bit into the leather. His fingers come back wet with blood. He rubs the tingling, numb wound beneath.

Tchk. Tchk. Tchk.

Chapter Twenty-Four

Grouchy

GROUCHY SCRATCHES THE DIAMOND quickly against the
wall while the humans' eyes dig into the back of his neck. Prison
taught him never to turn his back on danger. It also taught him
the importance of numbers in a fight. The humans outnumber the
dwarfs six to three.

Tchk. Tchk. Tchk.

Behind him, the captain says, "Tell us. How did you know
about destroying the creatures' brains? Is there anything else you
know about them?"

Snoozy tells them about fleeing the house, fighting off Blushful,
and then climbing up the tree. Of how the Prince grabbed him as
he climbed down. Damn it. The Prince still walks. Grouchy's blood
simmers. He stares at Snoozy.

"The Prince w-was so quiet." Snoozy's voice shakes. "A-all
smoke and snowflakes until he started moaning. He grabbed me. I
was rooted. So, I let go. It is autumn, after all. I fell on top of him
and wiggled free. Somehow, I grabbed his honey-gum." He pauses

126 | Rob E. Boley

to pop another piece of gum into his mouth. "As I ran away, there was Blushful, still lying on the ground. Popped bubble. Weightless. Waiting. Finally at peace. Stabbing his eye killed him. I went between the trees and found Grouchy and Merry." Snoozy looks to Merry now. "Their bags were outside the tent."

Snoozy's balled fists, sweaty forehead, compulsively-chewing jaw, and hunched soldiers tell Grouchy that the raylee root poison in his system is eating him alive.

Grouchy turns to his completed diagram. "Right. So, this is the mine. We're here."

He points at the staging chamber on the diagram, from which a passage extends deep into the mountainside and curves around the main deposit of ore inside the mountain. Where the passage begins curving around the ore, a deep shaft drops straight down a length taller than most trees. At the far end of the passage, another shaft drops down—but this shaft spirals in a coil. The shaft and the spiraling passage are connected below on three different levels. From these levels, additional passages are dug outward into the ore deposit. Essentially, the northwest passage looks like a bizarre step ladder—with one straight rail for the shaft, one twisted rail for the spiraling passage, and three rungs for the three lower levels.

"The spiral ramp has rails for a mine car," Grouchy says. "The shaft has a platform that can be lowered and raised from up top."

Tchk. Tchk. Tchk.

The captain tilts his head. "Okay, so what's the plan?"

Grouchy winds his finger down the spiral. "One group lures the Horrors down the spiral here to the lower levels. Another group caves-in the entrance to the spiral. A third group hauls up the first group using the vertical shaft's platform. The Horrors will be trapped. We have a raft at the other side of the mountain. It'll take us to Abundance. To Dr. Killington."

Monk strokes his mustache. "We've pulled off worse plans, Captain."

The captain frowns. "The Horrors can't get up the shaft?"

"Emergency rungs are built into the shaft. We'd have to pry them out from the bottom level using the lift."

"How do we cave-in the ramp?" Monk holds up a battered pickaxe. "These tools are about done."

"Dandelion," Snoozy says, eyes fixed on the floor. "Sun burst. Boom."

Tchk. Tchk. Tchk.

Grouchy nods. "We have explosives. But we'll have to retrieve them from the abandoned northeast passage."

Merry shakes his head and points at him. "Hold it one darned minute. How many plans do we have to watch go up in flames? *Let's put the Horrors in a bag. Let's put the Horrors in the cottage. Let's trap the Horrors in the mine.* No more. Let's finish this now. Battson is right. We should just slaughter them and be done with it."

The captain slams his fist into the rubble, raises his voice. "They're my soldiers, and they'll do as I say. And I say we try to contain these Horrors, then find a cure. Otherwise, our Queen will have all of our heads."

"Damn the Queen," Battson says. "I vote for killing these Horrors."

"I vote with you, Cap'n," Hays says.

"I vote for capturing them," the Page says, largely ignored.

Tchk. Tchk. Tchk.

"This is not a democracy," the captain says. "You don't get a vote. This is the Service."

Despite the fact that the captain agrees with his plan, anger boils in Grouchy's belly. The words bubble up his throat fueled by steam and hatred. "Like hells it is. This isn't the Service. It's our damn mine, not a battlefield. And you're not soldiers anymore. You're survivors, just like us."

"We should vote," Merry adds.

Battson nods. "Agreed. We should vote. But humans each get two votes, and the dwarfs each get one."

That's it. Balls to this. Grouchy hobbles over to Battson, his busted toe flaring with pain. "I'm finished with you, swob."

"Then finish me, stump."

"Battson, stand down or I will feed you to those Horrors outside." The captain's yell echoes down the mine. He takes a labored breath. "Boy, do you really think it's as easy as taking these monsters down one by one? You think you will be able to do that here in this dark, cramped cave? What if one slips through? In the Rice Wars, the dwarfs had suicide rebels that we called 'Dump-Stumps.'" He turns to the dwarfs. "No offense."

Grouchy spits. "Balls."

The captain turns back to Battson. "Know why we called them that? Because when you're fighting something that has nothing to lose, it's like having a big load of shit dumped on you. And right now, we've got a whole army of shit out there waiting to—"

The rubble behind Shrub and Monk shifts, and rock sprays in all directions. A mangled Horror emerges, its face a mess of torn flesh and cracked bone. It flails blindly, both its eyes now shattered cavities. The Page screams.

Shrub scoots off the pile, but the Horror falls on him, bites the back of his head. The soldier's head snaps backward. Monk swings his pickaxe and shatters the Horror's skull. Shrub hisses, jerks forward, and pulls back with Monk's right ear between his teeth. Monk screams, chokes, and hisses.

Grouchy unsheathes Honey-Stick.

Chapter Twenty-Five

Merry

FEAR FLUTTERS IN MERRY'S belly like a flaming moth. Just steps away, Monk and the hairy soldier, Shrub, scramble to their feet and hiss. Battson scoots backward, bumping into Merry and knocking him to one knee.

Behind him, the Page screams.

Shrub leaps at Merry, knocking him onto his back. It's the hardest he's ever been hit, and the first time he's been struck by a human. The impact knocks the wind out of his gut. His head strikes the floor, and stars blossom in his vision. He fumbles against Shrub's chest, but the Horror lowers its head. Shrub's hot, panting breath rakes at his beard.

At last, the darkness has won.

He whimpers. A metal blade flicks its tongue through Shrub's neck. The Horror's head falls from its shoulders and smacks Merry in the face. He shuts his mouth and wipes the cursed blood from his face.

Pushing Shrub's headless body away, he sits up in a daze.

Nearby, Hays hits Monk upside the head with a pickaxe.

But hot hands grasp Merry's chest. Shrub's headless body clambers over him. Fingers pinch and fumble his flesh, and he kicks the Horror backward. It stumbles onto its feet and into the wall, leaving a bloody smear over Grouchy's diagram. Blood jettisons out the open neck. Its hands clench and unclench as if grabbing chunks of air.

"Shit on me," Grouchy says with his typical eloquence.

Grouchy slams a fist-sized rock onto Shrub's severed head. The skull bursts open, and Shrub's body collapses like a puppet with snipped strings.

For a long while, the only noise is their heavy breathing and the Horrors' incessant digging. The sound tickles the back of Merry's brain, where darkness swirls and swells. That same darkness nests under his feet and dares him to take a step.

Tchk. Tchk. Tchk.

All around them, lantern-cast shadows wiggle and dance. Taunting Merry. Laughing at him. He reaches in his pocket for his worry stone, but it's gone. The soldiers took it—and the roots—back on the path.

Tchk. Tchk. Tchk.

Finally, the captain speaks. "I heard the gate break just before the cave-in. I guess one got in."

Hays coughs. "Lucky you didn't get bit, Cap'n."

The captain shakes his head. "Yeah, I'm lucky."

Merry wipes more blood and drool off of his face. The dark blood could have been bled by the night itself.

"Careful," Hays tells him. "Watch out for blood bugs."

"What?"

"Blood bugs. Little creatures that swim in blood. My sister Randa taught me that's how sickness gets passed, by blood bugs swimming from one person to another."

"Blood bugs." Battson scowls, shakes his head. "Shut up, pinky."

Tchk. Tchk. Tchk.

The captain addresses everyone, "Let's get going. No telling how long before those demons claw their way in."

"Agreed," Grouchy says. "I'll get the dinermite. Snoozy, can you prep the blasting caps and rig the fuses? Merry, can you work the lift and make sure those rungs get pulled?"

"Of course." Merry offers a grin.

At last, he's gaining Grouchy's respect. It really feels like Merry has become accepted as part of the dwarf family now that the family is falling apart. He doesn't agree with the current plan, but he's done meddling and politicking. If only he'd given Blushful that tea, maybe things would have gone differently. The core help him if Grouchy ever finds out. No matter. He can't change the past. He can only leave it buried in the darkness where it belongs.

"Grouchy, Battson's with you," the captain says.

"What?" Battson says, but the captain gives him a rusty dagger stare.

Hays and the captain agree to pry the rungs off the vertical shaft. The captain orders the Page to stay in the staging chamber and warn the others if the Horrors break through.

Tchk. Tchk. Tchk.

Everyone gathers pickaxes, fuses, rope, and other gear. The soldiers stack their dead neatly in the corner. Merry passes around the one canteen of water stored in the mine. Battson, of course, refuses to drink after the dwarfs.

Before the group splits up, Grouchy pulls Merry aside. "Merr, you saved my ass back there with the Prince."

Merry's smile widens, the corners of his mouth propping up his warmed cheeks. "It seemed like the thing to do."

"Well, be careful down there." Grouchy lowers his voice. "Take care of Snoozy. Don't trust the swobs."

"You're stuck with the foul one. The captain and the boy seem quite likable. I think under—"

"No." Grouchy's face hardens. "The swobs are our enemies. Don't ever forget that. They may seem nice enough now, but how long do you figure that'll last outside this mine?"

Grouchy pats Merry's belly and limps down the northeast passage with Battson.

Before Merry can duck into the northwest passage, Snoozy steps in his path. The heavy-eyed dwarf holds out one clenched fist, then opens it to reveal Merry's worry stone. Shiny and black, the stone looks like a hole in Snoozy's palm. Always, there's a hole. In every plan. In every day. In every moment. A hole that lets the darkness in.

"I thought you should have this," Snoozy says, his breath sweet with honey-gum.

Merry's stomach lurches. "Th-thank you, Snoozy."

"I found it in the bags," he says pointedly.

If Snoozy found the worry stone, he also found the raylee roots. He should tell the others that Snoozy has the roots—he knows Snoozy won't be able to control himself—but in doing so, he'd be revealing his own horrible deed.

"I'm . . . I'm sorry, Snoozy."

Hays approaches and asks Snoozy, "When you were in the woods earlier, did you see a dog? About this high?" He holds his hand at mid-thigh level.

With Snoozy distracted, Merry ducks into the passage.

Into the darkness.

Chapter Twenty-Six

Snoozy

THE SOLDIER, HAYS, PRATTLES about his dog, but Snoozy ignores him and instead watches Merry scurry away. Why didn't Merry give the roots to Blushful? What was that fat fool thinking? Snoozy shakes his head.

He clutches the roots—soft and gritty—in his fist. He shouldn't. Not now. Except that the hole in his belly grows so hard and unyielding, like this very mine. Dark. Empty. He swallows his gum, brings his fist to his mouth, and pulls one of the roots free with his teeth. It tastes like rich, spicy dirt. A cloud swirls in his head.

"I'm sorry," he says to Hays. "Could you repeat that?"

"A dog. Did you see a dog in the woods?"

Snoozy shakes his head, and rain cascades down his throat and into his belly. It fills the hole. "I didn't see anything."

Hays nods. "I sure hope she's okay out there."

"She'll be fine so long as she stays out of the rain."

"Rain? It's dry as a dusty cracker out there."

Snoozy giggles. The captain pulls Hays down the passage after

Merry, and Snoozy chews and laughs, chews and laughs.

Eventually, he follows, leaving the Page behind to watch the cave-in.

They walk a good while in the dark. Shadows throb. Snoozy pops another root, and soon a river pours down his throat and into his heart. The shadows undulate and squirm into a parade of torn flesh, leering eyes, leafless limbs, and skeletal birds. The captain and Hays stumble a few times in the writhing darkness, and Snoozy bites back a laugh.

Finally, Merry opens his lantern. "Sorry. I forget that you need more light." Now they reach the curve in the passage where the ceiling drops abruptly. Merry pats the ceiling. "Mind your heads."

Mine your heads. Head your mines.

The humans squat as they walk through the shortened passage. The scent of dust, grease, and burning lantern reminds Snoozy of his earlier vision of the burning tree. Wood patients. Would patience.

"So, what exactly is the Collective?" the captain asks. "And why live here—so far from the Dwarflands?"

"For Bones, it was a statement to the world," Merry says, taking his lecture tone. "Eventually, he would've published an account of our life here. He wanted to take the lowliest dwarfs—youths like us that were outcasts, even by dwarf standards—and make them productive citizens. To prove that dwarfs were more than just the lies printed about us. More and more, he'd been traveling away from the cabin for daytrips. I suspect he was scouting to recruit humans, to show that humans and dwarfs could live together."

The captain grunts. "What do you mean by outcasts?"

"Each of us faced our own horrors. That's what Bones called them."

"Personal demons," the captain says.

"I've had those," Hays says. "Were yours the little ones that cut your hair in the night and put nut butter in your ears?

"Hays," the captain says. "Your sister is a Horror herself."

"Each day, we'd work in the mines from sunrise to sunset," Merry says. "Each night, Bones worked with one of us on our horrors, our alone time. He'd do that six nights in a row, working with each of us one-on-one."

"And on the seventh night?"

Now Snoozy speaks up, talking around a wad of root. "On the seventh night, he rested. We all did. We'd build a fire and burn a tree. Down to the root. To the soil. To the stump. Seven merry stumps."

Merry cuts him off. "And you'd play songs on your flute. Beautiful songs."

"Doesn't sound like your man Bones got much rest," the captain says.

Snoozy laughs. "Not getting much now, either."

They walk the rest of the way to the vertical shaft in silence. There, Hays kicks a stone into the shaft. It bounces off the walls for a long time before reaching bottom—a distant ellipsis of noise.

Merry attaches the lantern to a hook anchored above one of the shaft's two lifts Each lift is suspended from a pulley mechanism and operated from a control station at the top of the shaft. That's where Merry goes. He fiddles with an assortment of weights and counterweights. Ropes slither and squirm like hairy worms.

The soldiers climb onto a lift, and Merry lowers it so that they are eye-level with the top of the shaft. They pull at the highest rung first.

"It's coming," says Hays, pulling with his pickaxe. "It's snug as a tick on a hairless bitch's belly."

Snoozy stands at the shaft's edge. "Careful. Don't let your pickaxe bite you."

"Wouldn't be your first bite, would it?" The captain's sweat-covered face grins. "Hays here has become our animal handler. He's a natural with animals—the furry ones, anyway. He's worthless with a fish."

"Now that's—" Hays starts, but the rung pops out of the wall and ricochets down the passage. A clattering symphony echoes through the mine. The noise jolts Snoozy's thoughts.

He turns to Merry. "I'm going to prep the fuses. Tie up all the loose ends."

Merry offers him a weak smile, but says nothing.

The soldiers are still struggling with the next rung when he walks further down the northwest passage. Soon, he reaches the top of the spiral.

If all goes according to plan, the explosion he's prepping will cave-in the ramp once the Horrors have been lured below—effectively trapping them. The only way out after the explosion would be climbing up the vertical shaft, which won't be an option once the soldiers pry out the rungs anchored into the shaft wall.

That's the plan, anyway. He pops another root into his mouth, jaws now working furiously on the growing clump. He stares down at the mess of fuses in his hands, watches them squirm with anticipation.

Chapter Twenty-Seven

Grouchy

GROUCHY LEADS BATTSON DOWN the abandoned northeast passage. He limps as quickly as he can, but his left toe, knee, and calf each flare with their own dandy brand of discomfort. The swob's lantern casts a long, flickering shadow of Grouchy on the ground in front of him. It's what he might look like if he were a swob: taller, slimmer.

Swobs, here in his mine. He grits his teeth and shakes his head. Of all the options, why did the captain send Battson with him?

"Why am I partnered with you?" Battson whines. "Why does that pinky Hays gets to be partnered with Captain?"

Grouchy grunts. "Maybe your captain is overwhelmed by your charm."

Battson ignores him, or perhaps isn't even listening. "Why the hell did you stumps store the damn explosives so far away?"

"Why do you swobs ask so many dumbass questions?"

The passage curves to the left, and the ceiling lowers abruptly to dwarf height. He doesn't bother warning Battson, just enjoys the satisfying *thump* as Battson smacks his head on cold rock.

"Shit."

Grouchy grins. "Watch your head. Wouldn't want to damage your girlishly pretty face."

"Watch your mouth, stump. I'm just saying. You're nothing special to me."

The passage's walls are rough and jagged, the ceiling more so. Battson crouches deep to keep from hitting his head again, which takes some of the pressure off of Grouchy to walk at the human's pace. Here, the mine smells mustier, like a secret. It's been closed for years, now used only for storing the dinermite.

Not much further, they come to an alcove overlooking a wide pit—the vertical shaft. Hungry shadows gobble up the rusted, crooked rungs embedded in the shaft's wall.

"How deep is it?" Battson asks.

Grouchy grunts. "Very."

"How do we get down?"

"Have you ever rappelled?"

"What, like insects?"

"Not repelled, ass-pit. *Rappelled.* With rope."

"Isn't there a platform to lower us?"

Grouchy shakes his head. "We scavenged its parts for the northwest passage's platform."

In abrupt sentences peppered with obscenities, he explains the basics of rappelling. He has two harnesses, both loose on Battson's slender waist. He demonstrates how to lean outward from the wall and how to position his hands—one holding the rope above him and one behind him feeding the rope into the harness. He ties two ropes—ragged as old dish towels—to rusted anchors embedded at the shaft's edge.

With the ropes in place, Battson grabs the rope as Grouchy

demonstrated and leans backward over the shaft. With a flick of Honey-Stick's blade, Grouchy could send him plummeting to a crunchy, sticky death. So why doesn't he?

"Shouldn't I have gloves?" Battson says, eyeing Grouchy's own mining gloves.

"Probably. Want to go back for some?"

Battson grits his teeth. "I don't like you."

"Good. Now go down. Like I showed you."

Battson feeds the rope into the harness and lets his body lean back further, almost horizontal. With mostly straight legs, he hops awkwardly down the shaft. Satisfied that the swob probably won't break his precious neck, Grouchy hangs a lantern over the shaft, leans over the edge, and rappels into the darkness.

He savors the sensation of falling, gently kicking off of the shaft's wall, and dropping in a long, lazy arc through the darkness. He feels like a feather falling into the darkness.

———— ◆ ————

THE FIRST AND ONLY time he saw Snow naked was in the darkness.

He and the dwarfs came home from the mine, and no delicious meal simmered on the stove. Snow was nowhere to be seen. His stomach immediately contracted. He was shocked at how scared he was for her. The others seemed less concerned.

He forced himself not to run, but to walk upstairs, then entered the loft wide-eyed. He waited for his pupils to expand in the darkness. Snow lay in the middle of the beds, only a light sheet covering her naked body. She snored lightly.

He averted his eyes. "Hello? We're home."

"Fists?" Her voice was sticky with sleep. "Is that you?"

He puffed out his chest at the word "Fists." That was her new nickname for him since he'd begun teaching her how to punch and kick using a gem sack full of dirt hanging from the oak tree in the backyard.

"Sorry to wake you, Snowflake. We got home, couldn't find you."

She sat up on one elbow. "I'm sorry. I must have dozed off." She blinked blindly.

"No. Sorry to wake you."

"I'm glad you did. I hate napping past nightfall. It's unnatural waking up in the dark. The darkness gets under your eyes and won't come out no matter how much you wake up."

Grouchy bowed his head. He'd slept, woken, and slept again in darkness much of his life. The darkness was in his bones.

"Oh, fump-sticks. I didn't make dinner. You poor fellas must be starving, working in the mines all day and imagining coming home to a great meal."

She sat up and the sheet fell, exposing her perfect breasts. Like ripe fruit. Grouchy's stomach growled. She swung off the beds, revealing her bare back and perfect ass. When she bent over to retrieve her dress, he nearly fell over.

He savored one final glance, then stepped out onto the staircase. He sniffed his armpits—rancid. Shit. He should've rinsed before finding her, but he'd been worried about her. If the Queen wanted Snow dead, there wasn't much that would keep that from happening.

Snow slipped past him and sat on the top step, slid her blue shoes onto her perfect little feet. Below, the dwarfs whistled to themselves as they stored their dirty clothes and washed at the sink. Merry scurried about, collecting the books, clothing, and other items that Snow had left lying about.

"I love the songs you fellas sing and whistle," she said.

"We whistle while we work to orient to each other in the dark mines."

"We whistle while we work," Snow echoed. "That'll twist your tongue in a knot."

Grouchy paused, his head stuck on her words "twist" and "tongue." He flexed his fingers. "You, uh, want to do some more training later, Snowflake?"

Snow held out her bruised knuckles. "It still hurts. I thought you were going to teach me how to not get hurt."

"I'm teaching you to defend yourself. That ain't the same as not getting hurt."

She smiled sideways at him. "That's stupid."

Grouchy laughed. "Fighting is stupid. Know why?"

"Why, Fists?"

"Because everyone gets hurt. Even if you win. I'm just teaching you how to get hurt less and hurt your attacker more. But there ain't no winning in a fight. You get in a fight, you've already lost. Everyone's a loser."

Snow sighed. "Story of my life."

He grunted a chuckle.

"Fists?"

"Yeah?"

She stared at him and brushed something out of his beard. "Who taught you how to fight?"

He bunched up his lips. "My father taught me. Just about every day of my life."

"That doesn't sound good."

"We lost Mother in the Rice Wars. I was just a baby. He raised me as best he could, but it wasn't easy. I was difficult. And he was, uh, busy."

"Doing what?"

"He was part of the resistance. He'd been a soldier in the Rice Wars—one of the best. And he never stopped fighting, even when the war ended. Even after I was born. Even after Mother died." His father, Kiel, was known for his ruthlessness. After a battle, he'd cut patches of skin from his human victims and use the patches to make a gruesome sash. Sometimes he whipped Grouchy with that human leather. "Some days, he'd hit me for no reason out of the blue—just to toughen me up. So that I'd be ready for anything. He used to poke me with a pencil to get me to yell."

"Why?"

"He said all warriors had to have a warrior yell. Something that came straight from their core, unfiltered. Pure power. He said he'd keep poking me until he heard me let out a real warrior yell."

"Why put you through all that?"

He shrugged. "Either to punish me or to teach me how to fight back."

"Fight back against him?"

He shook his head. "Against you."

Snow bowed her head. "My people have caused you a lot of pain."

He shrugged. "Sounds like they've caused you no small amount of pain, too."

———— ◆ ————

NO SMALL AMOUNT OF pain. It occurs to him now, as he bounds through the darkness, that pain is something they shared. Pain and resentment. And her life story, "everyone's a loser," is perhaps the reason he was so drawn to Snow. After all, in the dwarf townships, everyone is a loser. That's the story they all have in common, thanks to the swobs.

He wishes he'd had the courage to kiss her. To offer her his love. To take her far away—away from the Collective and Queen Adara and evil witches with nasty apples.

Not far below, Battson bounds off the wall.

"Coming past you, swob. Watch the hell out."

"Whatever, stump."

Grouchy passes the human. "I'll tell you when you're at the bottom."

He reaches the bottom just a couple bounds later, debates whether or not to warn Battson. Nah. Still in mid-rappel, Battson slams ass-first onto the bottom of the shaft.

"Ow," he shouts.

"Heh. You're at the bottom."

Battson's eyes narrow. "That wasn't funny. I could have broken my lantern." He gets to his feet—hands clenched in fists—but then something grunts down the passage. Nothing should be down here. "Damn you, stump. I'll—"

Grouchy holds up a palm. "Hush. You hear that?"

"Don't shush me, short-pants." Battson rubs his bruised ass. "You could have gotten me killed." Battson finally shuts up and follows Grouchy's ginger steps down the passage. "What did you hear?" Battson whispers, lighting his lantern.

"Not sure. But something's down here." He shivers under his sweat-soaked clothes and tucks his gloves back into his pockets.

"How much further to the explosives?" Battson asks.

He points down the passage. "In an alcove at the first branch."

"Is this passage safe? When's the last time you were down here?"

More damn questions. "About a moon ago. We turn the explosives every so often. Otherwise, they become unstable."

"Unstable. Great." Battson sniffs. "It smells like an animal. Do you smell it?"

Grouchy sniffs, but smells only dust. "Give me your lantern."

Battson hands the lantern over, and they continue down the passage. Grouchy keeps the lantern's pane covered with his palm so that only the slightest light escapes.

Near the alcove, Battson's boot smooshes into something on the ground. The lantern illuminates a large pile of dung.

"Is that what I think it is?" Battson says.

He straightens up and aims the lantern down the passage. The flickering light illuminates a furry bulk with two glowing eyes. The shape almost fills the width of the passage. Its claws scrape dully at the stone floor. A fumping bear.

"Yeah," Grouchy says. "It's the story of my life."

Chapter Twenty-Eight

Hays

HAYS AND THE CAPTAIN stand on the platform at the shaft's bottom, where they pry the lowest rungs from the shaft's wall. To one side, the lowest passage stretches into the darkness, presumably toward the spiral shaft. To the right and left of the shaft, alcoves extend several steps into the rock, probably so that the lifts can be loaded from multiple sides.

Goose pimples dot Hays' forearms. He flexes his pickaxe against the well, and out pops another rung. It clangs onto the lift, and he kicks it aside. "I gotta say, Cap'n. These dwarfs don't seem as bad as folks back home talk."

"Are you Hopish, Hays?" Captain asks.

Hays shrugs. "My Pappy believed all the old stories. He passed them onto my Pa, and my Pa passed them onto me. Pa didn't fully believe it, but he never would have told that to Minister Ramsizer. Pa said Moncansas had been at sea for so long they burned all historical records for fuel. So, Cap'n Hardoyan could make up whatever stories he wanted. And my Ma always said not to believe everything I hear. Course, she was probably talking more about my sister Randa. So, I guess my answer is that I'm not sure what to believe. I'm just trying to do right by my family and the world. I hear the Moncansas is still anchored in the bay at Carpaldal. Is that true, Cap'n?"

Captain nods. "The first arks were torn apart for firewood and to make new buildings. But the third ark still floats far off shore. Some of the Hopefuls try swimming out to it each year as some kind of pilgrimage. None ever make it, but the spectacle makes for good gambling." After a pause, he adds, "For those who would gamble on men's lives."

"Why all this talk of the Hopefuls, Cap'n?"

Captain wipes sweat from his brow even though he's clearly shivering. "You see a man come back from the dead, and it makes you wonder what's next. And speaking to your point, no, dwarfs aren't evil. We wronged them terribly by letting the Hopefuls set up their damned kingdom. And you know why we did it?"

Hays shakes his head.

"Politics. That's why. The Moncansas' abrupt arrival was like a rude, drunk uncle showing up to a wedding. He has to be accommodated, but no one really wants to sit with him. You have to understand that the Moncansas was at sea decades longer than the first two arks—an extra generation. With little hope of ever finding land, their Captain Hardoyan had to give his people something to believe in, so he created a new religion cobbled from children's bedtime stories, fever dreams, and some actual history."

Captain's going into one of his stories. That's fine by Hays. He enjoys Captain's perspective, the experience coming from so many far-off travels. Right now, though, Captain's breath stinks of sour milk. Hays turns his head away and listens. It's going to be awhile.

"According to that new religion, Hope, we had been sent in the

Arks out of the Heavens, a glorious land, through the Betweenplace of clouds to the World Below to prepare the World Below for its eventual Ascension. Once the World Below was cleansed of impurity, a brilliant white fire would engulf it, burning our bodies and raising our spirits to the Heavens. But this Ascension could only happen if the Hopeful converted the entire human populace to their beliefs and exterminated the wicked dwarfs."

Captain coughs and continues. "The Ascendio Kingdom was made because no one wanted that drunk uncle to stay at their house. When the Hopeful arrived, they made it their first priority to convert the Eastern and Western Kingdoms to their beliefs. Their second priority was the elimination of the dwarfs. The Eastern and Western Kingdoms debated long and hard about what to do with the Hopefuls. They finally decided to give them their own kingdom and to make Captain Hardoyan's direct descendants royalty.

"We pushed the dwarfs into a wasteland where we knew they couldn't survive. Yet somehow, they did. So what did we do? We put unsustainable quotas on their rice production. They had two choices: obey the kingdoms, export all their rice, and watch their families starve, or defy the kingdoms. I can tell you, that's no choice at all.

"Politically, it was a smart move. Establishing a new kingdom and purging the dwarfs distracted the Hopefuls from their work of cleansing the other kingdoms. Not everyone agreed, of course. The Western Kingdom's navy protested, and many of them became pirates. Like most political decisions, it was a temporary solution for a long-term problem. Because now the Ascendio Kingdom is at least as strong as our Kingdoms and is well on its way to forcing an all-out war against the dwarfs. And when that war's over, the Ascendio bastards will set their sights on us."

Coughing, Captain raises his pickaxe and taps the metal clamp fastening the lift to its rope.

Cling. Cling. Cling.

The soldiers wait in silence, taking quiet breaths. From above, the signal is answered.

Clung. Clung. Clung.

It's Merry, telling them that the lift is about to be raised.

"I've got to sit," Captain says, almost collapsing.

Odd. He's usually not one to let his age slow him down. Hays' pa was the same way—strong and sturdy, forged of rock and leather. Captain is like Hays' pa, but more fair. Pa always expected more from Hays than from his five sisters, Randa, Carmel, Starly, Pean, and Laven. Always.

The lift rises.

Hays' heart lowers.

Poor, lost Yanky.

Pa would shake his head and call him a damn fool, but Hays aches inside. He misses his dog, his best friend.

Named for her undying passion for playing tug-of-war, Yanky was one of the few gifts Pa ever gave Hays. It was on his twelfth birthday. Pa was trying to teach Hays responsibility. His sisters, especially Randa and Carmel, tried for years to woo Yanky away with treats and affections, but to no avail. Yanky and Hays spent countless hours exploring the remnants of forest surrounding the farm, hiking into Millet's Meadow, and playing fetch with Randa's dolls.

The lift jerks to a halt at the next set of rungs. Hays wedges his pickaxe under a rung, but Captain puts a trembling hand on his shoulder.

"Hays, I have something important to tell you." Captain pulls down his boot, revealing a jagged wound on his calf. "I've been bitten, son."

Hays shakes his head. "How? When?"

"I'd just pulled Cracker off of Battson and stabbed him—it. It seemed dead. Then it bit me. It barely broke the skin. I'm weak. Tingling. Cold. I'm dying."

Hays keeps shaking his head. He hasn't stopped since Captain's revelation. "It can't be."

"It can. It is. Deal with it." Captain squeezes his shoulders. "I'm promoting you to captain."

"Cap'n? No. No way. I'm not—"

"Yes, you are."

"What about Battson?"

Captain smiles. "You'd rather I promote him?"

"Hell, no. I mean, he won't take orders from me, Cap'n."

Captain rips his wing-shaped badge from his chest and places it in Hays' hand. Captain's flesh is as cold as the surrounding rock.

"Battson's arrogant and ignorant, but he's a damn good fighter. Whatever this thing is out there, you'll need him to contain it. Understand me?"

Hays nods.

"A word of advice. These wings don't put you above your men. Don't ever think otherwise. You provide your grunts with authority and guidance. You give them something to look up to, but don't think you're above them. Understand?"

Hays nods. "I do, Cap'n." He doesn't say the obvious—that unless he finds a cure for the infected Blumers, he's only in command of one soldier. And Battson gives not damn one about Hays' authority or guidance.

"I'm not your Cap'n, anymore, son. Now, you remember what I said. Otherwise you'll find yourself taking quite a fall."

"Yes, sir."

"Okay, Captain Hays, let's do this."

The soldiers pop loose another rung. Captain continues talking, his words scattered and ill-flowing, like that time Hays' sister Randa replaced Minister Ramsizer's sermon notecards with gibberish and crude jokes. What resulted was a sermon to remember, for sure.

"I can only imagine what'll happen if those things ever reach civilization." Captain faces Hays. "Contain it. Find a cure. Only then can you go home."

Hays nods.

Captain returns to the rungs. "I've still got lots of fire in this belly, so we stick to the plan. We'll lure those Horrors down here, but only you are coming back up. Got it?"

"Yes, Cap'n."

A rung pops. Captain continues.

"One more thing. When you get back to the Western Kingdom, go to the docks at Carpaldal. Find a ship called *Captain's Mate* and tell Darick that it was no one's fault but my own."

Hays nods. A rung pops. Captain continues.

"Say it back to me."

"I'll find the *Captain's Mate* and tell Darick that it was no one's fault but your own."

Captain reaches up for another rung, barely gets his pickaxe under it. "Say it again."

Hays does, more or less.

"Good man."

They strain against the rung, but it's too high for any leverage.

Captain shakes his head. "Let's move the lift upward. No sense killing ourselves." Chuckling wearily, he bangs his pickaxe on the lift wench.

Cling. Cling. Cling.

They wait for a response.

It doesn't come.

Hays looks up. Expects to see light from Merry's lantern. A firefly floating.

Instead, he sees darkness.

Chapter Twenty-Nine

Grouchy

A FUMPING BEAR. GRAND.

The furry mountain stands on all fours, too large to rise on its hind legs in the dwarf-sized passage. Its bulk consumes most of the passage's width, and its eyes glow pissy yellow in the lantern light. It lumbers forward, claws scraping long gashes in the dusty debris. Its perky ears are far too cute for such a menacing beast. The bear exhales through its flattened nose, and a hint of steam evaporates in front of its face.

Grouchy's stomach tightens as he whispers. "Don't look it in the eye. Slowly back the hells away. Show it we're not a threat."

"What about the explosives?"

Dammit. The swob's right. They need those explosives. Fortunately, the dead-end side passage is just a few steps away.

"Hells." Grouchy scoots forward. "Stay here. I'll get the explosives. If the bear charges, it's likely only bluffing."

"Likely?" Battson says.

"His way of telling us to get out of his damn cave. Don't

provoke it, swob. You don't want this fight."

Battson's furrowed brow tells Grouchy that he doesn't appreciate taking orders from a dwarf, but the jackass has enough sense to simply nod.

Watching the bear's feet, Grouchy inches toward the side passage. His heart pounds against his ribs, as if eager to escape. The bear grunts but stays put. A good damned sign. His wounded leg aches and throbs, but Grouchy tries stepping smoothly. No threat.

"Okay, Bear." He talks calmly, trying to sound like Merry. He even wears an idiot grin. "Sorry we entered your cave."

He ducks into the side passage. The explosives sit in a neat pile halfway down the passage against one wall.

"Just getting a few highly dangerous explosives. To capture some monsters."

The bear shuffles forward. Its furry bulk now blocks the passage entrance. Grouchy glances backward at the explosives. Another step, and the heel of his boot bumps a box.

Now is the most dangerous moment. If the bear charges, it could jar the dinermite. If even one box has become destabilized, the whole pile will blow.

"Just bending over, Mr. Bear. Need to grab a couple of boxes. Then I'll be on my way. No harm, no foul."

The bear's gigantic head sways side-to-side. It crouches, grunting a massive cloud of steam into the air.

Shit.

Balls.

Quick and powerful as an avalanche, the bear charges. Grouchy flattens himself against the wall, hoping the bear is bluffing. Sure enough, it shoots past him, but the beast's bulk knocks Grouchy backward onto the explosives. He closes his eyes, waits for the boom.

The explosion never comes.

The lantern tumbles from his hands. He catches it and hot metal sears his palm. He bites back a curse with clenched teeth, and eases the lantern onto his stomach. If he sees tomorrow, he will have blisters.

"Okay, Mr. Bear. I hear you. I'm leaving."

He climbs gingerly off the explosives. From the rear of the passage, the bear regards him with a tilted head. Its claws clack on the ground. Kneeling, Grouchy gathers two boxes of explosives, each the size of a brick but not quite as heavy. They smell like dusty bananas.

The bear follows as Grouchy eases backward. Battson waits in the main passage, and Grouchy hands him a box.

"We're leaving, Bear," Grouchy says. "Me and my human friend. Ever tasted human? Much better than dwarf. We're too tough."

Battson grunts. "I'm just saying, Mr. Bear. Everyone knows the best cuts of meat come from dwarfs."

The bear's head sways from side to side.

"Mother-fumping hells," Grouchy whispers. "It's going to charge. Be still. It'll either stop or run past. Protect the explosives. Don't antagonize the bear."

"You must be—"

The bear grunts, lurches forward, but stops just short of trampling them—close enough that he can smell the beast's rancid breath. It's another bluff. Everything's fine.

Except Battson yells and swings his sword at the beast's thick bulk. The bear roars—a noise that shakes Grouchy's toe bones. He grabs a fistful of dirt and pebbles from the ground. He throws a cloud into the bear's face—an old prison trick. The beast roars again, simultaneously sneezing and swiping a mighty paw across its

156 | ROB E. BOLEY

face.

Grouchy and Battson haul ass down the passage. Battson reaches the shaft first and jumps onto the rungs, scaling them with irritating grace. Grouchy stuffs his dinermite into his pants and clamps his lantern to his belt, then pulls himself upward. His broken fingers jolt with pain. His injured leg dangles uselessly as he hops up the rungs.

Below, the bear charges into the shaft, swings a massive paw upward, and swipes Grouchy's left foot clean off.

Damn.

Mouth gaping open, Grouchy watches as his boot strikes the ground. Oddly, there's no blood. Not even any pain. He looks down. There, attached to the end of his left ankle, is his foot. His wonderful, stinky foot—broken toe and all.

He sighs. "Holy hells."

He hops up one more rung, now safely out of reach. Blood drips from his bare foot and splatters onto the bear's muzzle. Its claws must have slashed more than just his boot.

"Hey, swob," he says. "What part of *don't antagonize the bear* was too fumping vague?"

Battson simply chuckles.

The bear *hmphfs* at them.

It's a long climb back to the top of the passage, especially with one bad leg and a brick of dinermite. What he wouldn't give for some sleep right now. Deep, deep slumber. The last time he slept deep was moons ago—the night of his last conversation with Snow.

———— ◆ ————

SHE FOUND HIM IN the night, asleep at the top of the staircase. He was trying to get a few winks before sunrise.

Snow shook him awake. "Fists, is that you?"

"You okay, Snowflake?" he whispered.

"I was just getting a drink."

"I'm a bit thirsty myself."

"Wait right here." She patted his belly, a habit she'd learned from the dwarfs.

Grouchy shuddered inwardly at her touch. She padded down the stairs, a ghost in her thin sheet. Her feet were delicate petals fluttering across the wood. She went through the kitchen and out the back door. Why? Maybe she had to pee.

Shortly, she returned carrying a ceramic mug the size of her face. She handed it to him, and he took a mighty gulp. He promptly choked. It tasted like sour apples soaked in cooking oil. He forced it down.

Snow giggled. "I should have warned you."

"What the hells? What is that?"

"Apple whiskey."

Grouchy gave her back the mug. "Doesn't taste like any whiskey I've ever had."

She took a generous sip and smiled. "Don't look at me. I didn't make it."

Grouchy looked down at his sleeping comrades. "Snoozy. That little spud has a still, doesn't he?"

Snow took another sip. "My lips are sealed."

"You do this often, Snowflake? Drink apple whiskey while we sleep?"

"No. I really was just getting up for water. But I saw you here and figured we'd make it an occasion. One thing you learn working in the Chamber House kitchen—you make your own occasions. You're sure as shit not invited to anyone else's."

As she spoke, Grouchy drank in every inch of her luminous skin. They sat shoulder-to-shoulder, and her scent of strawberries and cream intoxicated him.

She handed him the mug. "What about you? You make it a habit, sleeping outside my door?"

Grouchy shrugged, drank, and winced. His head reeled—more from her touch than the drink. "Most dwarfs don't snore, but Bones could stun a mule with his throat drumming."

Snow laughed. "Sometimes I hear it from upstairs."

"The others are stiff sleepers. Not me. My eyelids flutter all night long."

"Is that from your time in prison?"

"I guess."

"Why were you in prison? Did you hurt someone?"

Grouchy shook his head, took a drink.

"Did you steal something?"

Another drink. "I was in the wrong place at the wrong time."

She took the mug and nodded, a subtle gesture like a flower dipping under the weight of a bee. "Story of my life. I get that. Maybe that's why the Queen hates me so. Maybe I was in the wrong place at the wrong time."

"You didn't serve her any of this apple whiskey, did you?"

Snow snorted and shook her head.

"Too much salt in the royal soup?"

Snow shook her head again, took another drink.

Grouchy shrugged. "Maybe it's horse shit. Maybe that Head Huntsman lied. Maybe he had his own plans for you."

"Shit on a cracker, Fists. Now there's a cheerful thought."

They sat there a long while, trading stories and sipping that noxious concoction. She told him about life in the kitchen. He wanted to tell her about prison, but instead talked about the early days of the Collective—building the cottage and digging the mine.

Late in the night, she held his head in her lap and ran her

delicate fingers through his scraggly hair. He pretended to be asleep, hoping the moment would last forever.

"I hope one day you forgive me, Fists," she whispered. A stiff swallow followed. The young lass could certainly hold her liquor.

"Forgive you for what?" he wanted to ask, but the cottage swirled lazily around him. The apple whiskey rode thick in his veins. His belly twisted in and out of itself like two fat snakes consuming each other. Grouchy rolled his head back against her breasts. He clutched Snow's knee. She patted his hand.

Was her heart speeding up, or was that his heartbeat? It was his chance to show her how much he loved her. To kiss her. Surely, when she felt the intensity of Grouchy's kiss, she would hunger for him. Surely.

He rolled off of her lap, tried to sit up. The cottage wobbled like the flight of a wounded bird on a windy day. That flight—along with Grouchy's night— ended with a crash into darkness.

The next time he saw Snow, she was in a cursed sleep on the cottage floor—flat on her back.

———— ◆ ————

AND THAT'S EXACTLY HOW he finds Battson when he finally climbs over the top of the shaft—flat on his back. The young swob is stretched out, his hands behind his head. The box of dinermite sits nearby.

"Don't let me interrupt your beauty sleep," Grouchy says, sliding his own box of dinermite next to Battson's. "You sure as hells need all you can get." Grouchy throws himself onto the ground.

"How's your foot, stump?"

"You really give a shit?"

"Not even a little. Better hope big furry doesn't learn how to climb. Just saying. He's got your taste now."

Grouchy half-grins, glancing at Battson. His grin dries up quick. This boy's ancestors did horrible things to dwarfs. And they're still doing horrible things. He sits up. "Fump it. Let's go."

He wraps a rag around his bare foot before they head back toward the staging chamber. More than halfway there, Battson stops, leans against the wall, and takes a deep breath. The swob digs in his pocket and pulls out Grouchy's pipe and tobacco pouch.

Grouchy feels his eyes spring upward. "My pipe."

"Here," Battson hands it to him. "Let's take a break. I'm winded. We have time, right?"

"Beautiful idea." Grouchy sits down and rewraps his foot.

Battson sniffs Grouchy's pouch. "This isn't puddleweed, is it?"

"Balls to that. Tobacco with a hint of orange."

Without asking, Battson pinches some tobacco for himself, then hands the pouch to Grouchy. The dwarf stuffs his pipe while Battson pulls out a wide rolling paper and rolls himself a rumpel. Soon, they are both puffing away, filling the mine with smoke.

Grouchy eyes the burning stick of tobacco between Battson's fingers. Leave it to swobs to take a ritual as elegant as pipe-smoking and turn it into something so vulgar. "Why do you swobs call those things rumpels?"

The boy shrugs. "They're named after the man who first introduced tobacco to the Western Kingdom. He was quite the businessman. They said he was so smart that he could turn straw into gold."

"Yeah? What happened to him?"

"Legend has it he got in over his head. Got into some shady business with the queen at the time."

Grouchy grunts. "You swobs and your damn royals."

"You should have seen it," Battson says.

"What's that?"

"The look on your face when the bear clawed off your boot."

"Hmphf." Grouchy puffs out an angry cloud but soon chuckles. "Thought the damn thing had taken my foot."

Battson laughs. "He was a big bastard."

"Yeah. I guess that's why you screamed like a girl and tried to stab it."

"Bluffing my ass."

They both laugh, causing the smoke to swirl like a storm cloud. Grouchy's sides begin to ache, which only makes him laugh all the louder. He imagines what his father would say, to see him sitting here sharing a belly laugh with a swob soldier. That thought brings an end to his laughter.

"So, swob," he says finally, "all the other soldiers have darling nicknames like Monk and Cracker. What about you and Hays?"

"Hays is short for Hayseed. On account of him being a dumb hick."

"Ah. What about you?"

"Me? I'm just Battson. That's all. I'd ask about your name, but I think I have a vague notion why they call you Grouchy."

"Hmm."

"Long as we're interrogating the enemy, I have a question for you. Do you dwarfs have any theories about where the arks came from?"

Grouchy shrugs. "What do you care what we think?"

"I don't. But it's a mystery that all of us ponder. All the more mysterious is why none of our adults care. We soldiers aren't even allowed to talk about it. I can feel it happening to me—the not caring. It's like the curiosity is a wound in my brain that's slowly clotting over."

Grouchy's about to offer Battson some insights about how to

162 | ROB E. BOLEY

reopen his wounded brain when he notices the smoke begin swirling lazily down the passage—away from the mine's entrance. He feels a breeze—a tickle in his beard. He puts a hand on Battson's stomach. The swob immediately swats his hand like a gnat.

"What the hell, stump?"

Grouchy's belly squirms. "You feel that breeze?"

"Yeah. So?"

"So, there ain't no breeze in here." He gets to his feet and pockets his pipe. "The entrance is open. We're too late. The Horrors are inside the mine."

Chapter Thirty

Merry

MERRY SITS NEXT TO the lift, waiting for the soldiers' signal. Dust sprinkles the cool air. He rubs his aching back, ignoring his growling belly. Wipes his tired eyes.

At first, he's happy to be alone, to have time to think. He strokes his worry stone between his fingers and thumb, using a pattern similar to a finger snap. Most days, the stone serves as a talisman, attracting brilliant notions and inspirations. Easy as a snap.

Snap. Snap.

Not today.

Today, his thoughts spiral blindly in the darkness. The worry stone is the hole in things—the question that won't be answered. The answer that can't be faced. The face of all his fears. The fears that he struggles to question.

Assuming this plan succeeds, what happens next? With only three surviving dwarfs and the cottage reduced to ashes, will the Collective simply fall apart? And what of Snoozy, who has the raylee roots again? What's to stop the herb fiend from telling

Grouchy about Merry's dark deeds? His only hope is that Snoozy might perish, leaving his secret appropriately buried—and what sort of hope is that? Has the day not seen enough death?

Thud.

From down the passage—toward the mine's entrance—comes a noise.

Merry jumps to his feet, pockets his stone. He glances down the shaft, where the soldiers' dim light glows. He'll just investigate, then come right back.

He hurries down the passage toward the staging chamber. Up ahead, something's sprawled on the ground. Is it mining clothes? Gem sacks? No, it's the Page—flat on his back, right where the passage drops to dwarf height. On his forehead, a walnut-sized bump swells.

Merry kneels next to the Page and jostles him. "You okay?"

The Page stirs, licks his lips.

Merry repeats, "Everything okay?"

"No." Cobb holds his forehead. "I tried to warn you. I must have hit my—"

"Warn me?" Darn this foppish human. Is this what Grouchy feels like when talking to him? "What's happened?"

"They've broken through. It was so horrib—"

Merry yanks the Page to his feet and yells, "Come."

From down the passage toward him, merciless feet pound. Unrelenting hisses echo. Cobb picks up his sword with a trembling hand. Merry tugs him forward, the human's temple again striking the rocky ceiling.

"Come on, darn it."

More than once, the Page spills onto his hands and knees. All the while, the Horrors loom closer. Soon, he and the Page—both panting for breath—reach the vertical shaft. He rings a large bell, the one that Bones always used for meal breaks.

KUHH-KLLLANGGG.

His stomach growls at the noise. He almost laughs at his well-trained belly until the Horrors come into view.

Some of the soldiers have bloody stumps where their hands should be—likely from digging through the rubble. Most all display crusted bite and stab wounds. A shirtless, tattooed soldier leads the pack, his skin covered in ink, gore, and blood.

"Up," Merry urges. "Quickly."

Heart thumping, he hoists himself onto the remaining lift and climbs up the cat's cradle of ropes connecting it to the central pulley mechanism. The ropes stink of grease and dust. The whole structure sways under his weight, and his sweaty hands grip tightly.

He glances below at the Page, who tries to climb away from the mob. The tattooed soldier leaps and grabs the human's ankle. The Page shrieks and flails his sword in all directions.

"Don't…" Merry says.

But the Pages' frantic slicing cuts through two ropes and compromises the entire system. Ropes snap and unwind, and the Page falls into the mob of Horrors. Merry looks away from the slaughter but can't hide from the screams and crunching noises.

Above, a rope snaps. And another. The lift lurches, then collapses into the vertical shaft like a bucket into a well. Merry's stomach flip-flops into the darkness. And though he hasn't taken a breath, somehow Merry screams.

Snap. Snap.

Chapter Thirty-One

Grouchy

GROUCHY AND BATTSON RUN toward the staging chamber, and their swaying lanterns cast bizarre, lilting silhouettes. Grouchy almost slams into Battson when they reach the chamber. Ahead, four undead soldiers stand inside the chamber. A fifth clambers through a tunnel in the rubble, its edges splattered with blood and bone fragments.

Thick blood covers the soldiers' bodies, glistening black in the lantern light. One is missing half its face, revealing an eye socket and the skull beneath. Another has a broken jaw tilted horribly to the right. The third has no visible wounds, but a line of bloody drool hangs from its lower lip. The fourth's nose is broken. Blood drips like fudge from a tattered hole in its neck. The Horrors shamble as quiet as shadows towards them.

"Damn it," Battson says.

"Yeah."

Battson swings his sword at the nearest ghoul, Half-Face, separating head from body. It falls to its knees and tips forward toward Battson, its arms flailing blindly. Battson tries to sidestep but stumbles over a gem sack. The Horror's body lands on top of him.

The other three ghouls advance. Grouchy unsheathes Honey-Stick and stabs it through Fudge-Hole's mouth. The Horror lurches backward and collapses, yanking the sword right out of his hands.

Drooler and Broke-Jaw stagger toward Battson, who's now pinned under Half-Face's headless body. Both terrors fall to their knees to feast on Battson.

"Balls," Grouchy says, snatching Honey-Stick from Fudge-Hole's mouth.

With a slightly squeaky roar, he swings his blade through Drooler and Broke-Jaw's necks. It occurs to him then that killing Horrors is a lot like mining. You just swing and swing until you get your reward. Only in this case, the reward is life. Or, at least, a few more breaths.

KUHH-KLLLANGGG.

The noise echoes from the northwest passage. At the sound of the meal bell, Grouchy's belly growls. He almost punches his own stomach. What a time to think of food.

Around him, the three headless humans writhe and grasp on the floor. Battson scampers away from them, his mouth twisted in disgust. Across the room, rubble trickles down as the fifth Horror emerges from the blood-soaked tunnel. As the undead thing lurches to its feet, Grouchy's stomach twists.

It's the Prince.

Chapter Thirty-Two

Snoozy

SNOOZY SITS AT THE top of the spiral passage, stares at the undulating shadows. He stuffs another root into his mouth, where a well-worn wad already waits. His numb gums tingle and his teeth work steadily at the gritty, glorious glob. He fumbles with the long fuses, swats them when they wiggle or snap their teeth at him. He's already drilled holes in the wall and ceiling, each big enough for one stick of explosives. Bubble. Seed. Boom.

At first, the noises do not jar the thick syrup between his ears.

Not the horrified screaming.

Not the pounding feet.

KUHH-KLLLANGGG. Not even the meal bell, though his belly does stir at the sound.

No, these noises simply fizzle in the background like the smell of his own beard or the evening songs of crickets that become the fuzzy tapestry behind all summer memories.

Nearby, the mining cart—a large metal box on four wheels used to transport ore, gems, and dwarfs down the spiral passage—squats on parallel rails running the length of the spiral. At each of the mine's three lower levels, the dwarfs have installed a rail switch to divert the cart from the spiral onto rails running all the way to the vertical shaft. Snoozy's lantern hangs from a hooked metal pole that extends upward from one side of the cart.

Whistling, he twists the cotton string fuses around his fingers, making an elaborate web. A net. Cabin net. By candlelight, there's no boundary between his flesh and the rock walls, between the lines on his burnt palms and the fuses.

He is of the cave.

In the cave.

Within the cave.

Wait. Now he's not in a cave at all. The dark walls are rotted fruit. He's inside an apple hanging on a tree. Weight. The sickeningly sweet air contrasts horribly with the earthy spice of the roots in his open mouth.

A line of drool pools in one of his open palms. Gradually, he recognizes the distant hissing, screaming, and pounding not as sounds, but as colors spilling inside his skull and infusing his senses.

A terrible crash jars him.

It sounds as if the mine just broke its spine. He drops his web of fuses and rises, stuffing the extra fuses and his last root into his pocket.

Has the tree fallen? Has the apple fallen? The world is upside down. Sour juices ooze out of the rotten walls, pooling at his feet. He tries to run, but he's stuck at the apple's core.

He staggers toward the vertical shaft, but then hears desperate screaming. Patience. A raspy hiss bounces down the passage, seemingly aimed at him. Several Horrors emerge from the darkness. Patients. They move as one undulating mass of legs and arms, a tangled mess of worms scrambling toward Snoozy.

Turning, Snoozy runs, throws himself into the cart. He slaps the brake lever as he lands. His forward momentum shoves the cart down the spiral passage.

Now he's a seed tumbling inside the apple that's rolling down a hill. No, he is inside the seed, trapped in this smothering shell as strong as iron. Outside the shell outside the rotted fruit outside the apple's horrid skin, the spinning world is filled with hungry worms—eager to devour and shit and devour and shit still more. And here's one now.

A soldier Horror leaps onto the descending cart's rear, hanging onto the metal with gore-encrusted fingers. It hisses and snaps with its bloody mouth, its cheek torn open to expose gnashing teeth. Red spittle lands on Snoozy's pants, hot even through the heavy fabric.

The cart picks up speed. The lantern swings frantically. Erratic shadows undulate on blurry, glittering stones. Below, wheels screech against the tracks. The Horror's head smacks against the low ceiling. The soldier snarls. Worms pour out of its nostrils. Maggots writhe in its mouth. The grisly soldier grabs for Snoozy with one hand. Snoozy stomps the other hand. The Horror grasps the brake. Snoozy kicks harder. The monster hisses. Loses its grip. It splats into the rocky wall. The cart zooms downward, now leaning on two wheels. Snoozy reaches for the brake, but it's gone.

There's no stopping him now.

The cart tears into the spiral's final curve, and he pushes all his weight to the inside to keep the cart from tipping. The walls flicker past as a twirling river of sparkling stone. When the cart finally dashes into the lower level, something blocks the tracks up ahead.

It's Hays.

Chapter Thirty-Three

Grouchy

YESTERMORN, PRINCE MIKAEL WAS a well-dressed dandy-ass. Now, blood stains his cape and sticky gore covers his boots. His own innards coat his shredded silk shirt. His head tilts dramatically on his torn neck.

The Prince moans, a surprisingly infantile noise. Grouchy almost laughs. The headless corpses writhing on the floor only intensify the absurdity of the situation.

Half-Face's corpse grabs his boot, earning a bone-crunching stomp from Grouchy's bare foot. A bolt of lightning pain shoots down his shinbone into his ankle. He yells, barely catching himself on the wall.

"Shit." Grouchy rubs his foot. "Twisted my ankle."

Battson gestures at the Prince with his sword. "What the hell should I do?"

The Prince lumbers toward them, looking so pathetic that Grouchy can't even muster the hatred needed to finish him off.

He shrugs. "He's your fumping Prince. I'm sick of killing him."

Sighing, Battson jabs his sword unceremoniously through the Prince's eye. His remaining eye stares stupidly at the blade before he falls to his knees and flops to the ground.

Battson wipes his blade on the nearest gem sack. "I'm just saying. He's not my fumping Prince anymore."

The human grins at him, and Grouchy can't help but smile back. Clearly, they share a deep grudge against the world. Grouchy's grudge is against the Queen who cursed Snow and the humans who persecuted his people, and against the humans' anti-dwarf bigotry that keeps him apart from Snow. What's Battson's grudge, and why does he hate dwarfs so much? These questions will have to wait.

He stabs Honey-Stick through the three decapitated heads one by one, and the three writhing bodies go still. He yanks a boot off of the largest of the corpses and forces his bare foot into it. *Balls. How can these humans be so tall yet walk around on such narrow feet?*

"Come on then, swob." He limps down the northwest passage. "Let's damn well save the day."

Chapter Thirty-Four

Hays

THE LAST THING HAYS remembers is Captain shoving him off the lift. He smacked onto the cold ground at the bottom of the shaft, then instinctively rolled down the passage. Before he could take a breath, a tidal wave of rock smashed to the ground with a deafening roar. The impact shook the walls and extinguished the lantern.

Now he's immersed in darkness. Dust fills the air, causing him to cough and choke with each breath. Scrambling in the dark, he finds two metal rails running parallel to each other. Must be the rails for the mining cart. They should lead him to the spiral passage.

Before leaving the rubble, he shouts, "Cap'n? Cap'n?"

No reply. Hays pulls a length of thick rope out of wreckage, which as far as he can tell fills the full height of the passage. Damn. He'll have to take the spiral to the next level and see if he can find Captain from above.

At first, he crawls along the rails. Further from the debris, the air clears. He rises and takes tentative steps. Up ahead, a shrill noise tears through the mine. Sounds like a fairy-tale dragon screaming.

It's coming closer.

Dim light from above the spiral passage glows brighter with each step. The noise becomes more distinct—metal scraping against metal. He's only a few paces from the spiral when the cart whirls around the bend. His mouth drops open.

Snoozy sits in the cart and peers wide-eyed, his bearded face frozen in terror.

Nuts.

The passage is too narrow for him to dodge. Hays turns on his heel and sprints back the way he came, dragging the length of rope behind him.

The cart screams toward him, sounding like rusty barbed wire scraping across a slate. Suddenly, his rope goes taut, jerks him off-balance. He trips over the rails. The cart's front wheels have struck the rope. It lurches, jumps the tracks, wobbles to one side, snags the wall, and spills sideways.

Sparks shower as the cart slides forward. Screaming, Snoozy huddles inside the cart, limbs splayed stiff. Hays scampers backward on his ass. The urgent scent of hot metal and sparks fills his nostrils. He braces for the impact.

Except it never comes.

The cart grinds to a halt close enough that Hays can reach out and pat the thick metal. Somehow, Snoozy's candle lantern remains lit. It sways back and forth, alternately illuminating each side of the dwarf's face.

Hays pants. "We gotta get up top. The shaft caved in. Cap'n threw me off at the last second. We gotta rescue him."

Snoozy shakes his head. "Horrors spilling. Worms for the seeds."

"Is there another way up?"

Snoozy's head hasn't stopped shaking. "The spiral. Against the tide. Horrors like blood. Like sap."

"Like hell."

He pulls Snoozy out of the cart and grabs the lantern. When they reach the spiral, the Horrors' clamor above, an erratic symphony of footsteps and hisses. He sprints upward, dragging the dwarf. Their only chance is to reach the next level before the Horrors.

Around every bend, he expects his fiendish former comrades to attack. He chokes back a cough, his lungs full of splinters and dust.

When they reach the second level, Tattoo lurches around the bend. Now bare-chested and panting like a rabid dog, Tattoo cocks his head and hisses. Blood and drool spray into the air. Snoozy grabs the lantern from Hays and hurls it at Tattoo's head. The lantern bonks Tattoo's forehead, then smacks onto the ground.

The passage goes almost entirely dark.

Snoozy tugs him Hays down the passage, away from Tattoo's flailing and hissing, and away from more footsteps racing downward.

"I can see," Snoozy says. "Better than them."

He lets the dwarf pull him for a long, dark eternity. He crouches, but still smacks his head a few times on the ceiling. The darkness is as thick as an axe and just as threatening. Behind them, the Horrors' thrashing and pounding grows louder and louder.

"We're almost there," Snoozy says.

"Almost where?"

Snoozy skids to a stop. "The vertical shaft. Hollow. Nowhere to go but up."

"How?"

"Throw me across. Looks like you left enough rungs."

"What?" Hays shakes his head, a futile gesture in the dark.

"Dwarfs aren't great jumpers. But if you throw me across, I'll grab the rungs and light a fuse, so you can see where to jump."

"Hell, no."

"You have a better idea?"

He doesn't. So, he grabs the dwarf awkwardly, apologizing when his hand brushes Snoozy's crotch. The ceiling's still too low to stand completely upright, making for a difficult throw. He grasps the dwarf sideways by the shoulder and belt and counts down.

"This is it. Three."

Hays coughs and pivots.

"Two."

Spins around.

"One."

Tosses Snoozy into the darkness. His ears strain for any indication of the dwarf's fate, fully expecting to hear a splat followed by a thud below.

Finally, a squeaky voice comes from the darkness. "I made it. Hang on."

Skritch. Skritch.

A flame gasps to life. After a moment, it sparks even brighter. Across the shaft, Snoozy holds a lit fuse. Hays has never been so happy to see fire. Behind him, the mob's hissing grows louder. They can see the fuse, too.

"Good job, Snoozy." He takes a few steps back and whispers, "Here I go, Cap'n."

He launches himself across the shaft, but his last step lands awkwardly at the shaft's overhang. Flailing, he slams into the wall, knocking the breath from his bones. He catches the last rung, which pops halfway out of the wall.

With one hand clenched on the dislodged rung, his legs dangle. Flecks of stone fall into his wide eyes. The rung shifts yet again, one end now completely out of the wall. It's the last rung he and

Cap'n worked on.

No sense killing ourselves.

The rung now grits against rock. Metal bites into his hand. Holding his breath, he feels the rung on the verge of breaking free.

He flexes his bicep, slowly pulls himself upward. His muscles burn. The metal gives a little more, and bits of rock sprinkle onto his open eyes. He blinks them away and reaches upward with his free hand.

At last, he grabs the next rung and takes a grateful breath. He coughs, then whispers, "I got it, Cap'n."

"What's that?" Snoozy says.

"Nothing. Doesn't matter."

The fuse burns out, and darkness shrouds them. He climbs, hand over hand, until finally his feet step on the bottom rung. They climb silently, not wanting to attract the attention of the Horrors. A few rungs later, feet scuffle below. Something slams into the wall.

Snoozy strikes another match. Below, a soldier with a torn face hangs from the rungs and stares up at them with wide eyes— eclipsed moons floating in a blood-red sky. It lunges, grabbing for Hays' boot.

Chapter Thirty-Five

Grouchy

GROUCHY HOLDS HONEY-STICK AT the ready as he and Battson jog down the northwest passage. Up ahead, a ruckus simmers in the distance.

"What's that noise?" Battson says.

Grouchy shrugs and dims his lantern. When they reach the bend where the ceiling drops, he smiles, waiting for the thud of swob head on rock. Except as Battson approaches, Grouchy surprises himself by warning Battson.

"Duck, swob."

Battson grunts in appreciation.

Soon they arrive at the vertical shaft. Where once two lifts hung over the shaft, now a tangled mess of cut ropes dangle from pulleys. Gore covers the floor. The coppery scent of blood and burnt grease fills Grouchy's nose and tapers into his throat.

"What the hell happened?" Battson kicks dust across a blood puddle.

"Those fumping Horrors happened." Grouchy holds his lantern

over the shaft, illuminating darkness and several pairs of holes in the wall.

"The upper rungs are missing. At least that's gone right."

"Help!" a human shouts from below. "Who's up there?"

It's the young farmer-soldier. *What's his name?*

"Hays," Battson yells. "It's Battson and Grumpy."

"Grouchy, dammit."

"Same difference," Battson murmurs. He yells below. "I'll find something to pull you up."

"Hurry," Snoozy says. "The worms are boiling over."

Grouchy grins. Relief swells in his stomach. For a moment, he thought he was the last dwarf left. "Get your ass up here, Snoozy. We've got the bloody explosives. We'll lower a rope." He turns to Battson. "You get some rope at the staging chamber. Pull them up here. I'll blow the spiral shaft. The spuds will be trapped."

Battson nods and jogs down the passage, but Grouchy calls out his name. When Battson turns around, Grouchy grins.

"Watch your head, swob."

"Watch your ass, stump."

Grouchy limps toward the spiral, practically dragging his left leg. He finds that Snoozy has drilled the holes for the explosives running along the wall from the floor up to the ceiling and back down to the floor on the opposite wall. It's a wobbly pattern, but it'll do. Snoozy has already tied the fuses, now trampled on the ground.

He sheaths Honey-Stick, unwraps the two dinermite bricks, separates them into sticks, and then stuffs one into each hole. Ignoring the bitching pain in his busted fingers, he attaches a fuse to each stick making a rather shabby-looking spider web stretching across the spiral's entrance. He runs a central fuse several paces away. Down on his good knee, he lights a match and looks back at the spiral. When he sees her on the other side of the fuses, his mouth drops open.

It's Snow.

Chapter Thirty-Six

Battson

BATTSON SKIDS TO A stop in the staging chamber. He leans
on the wall and gasps at the musty air—his lungs now tired fists
grasping at strands of hair. He steps over beheaded bodies and
smashed skulls. A cramp chews at his ribs. Rummaging through a
trunk, he finds a knotted rope as thick as his thumb. He's about to
run back to the shaft, but the tunnel the Horrors dug through the
cave-in catches his eye.

He crouches before the tunnel but sees only darkness. Odd. It
should be early morning by now. He leans into the tunnel's blood-
sticky entrance, eager for fresh air. It stinks of gore and worse.

A stubby hand reaches through the darkness, and scraggly nails
gouge his palms.

With an unmanly gasp that, happily, no uncursed ears can hear,
Battson tumbles backward onto his ass.

The Horror hisses.

He holds up his lantern and illuminates a dwarf Horror. Ash and
gore cover its body, which is too wide for the tunnel. Glass shards

protrude from its plump cheeks. Bent glasses sit crooked on its nose.

Battson turns away, grasps a fist-sized rock, and chucks it into the tunnel. The motion is punctuated by a meaty thud. The dwarf hisses. Laughing under his breath, Battson sprints back down the passage. Never hurts to pause and enjoy life's little happy moments.

A quick sprint later, he's back at the vertical shaft. He unwinds the rope into the deep hole. His lantern reveals that the dwarf in the pit—Sleepy. Or Snoozy? Or Snorey? Whatever. — has almost reached the highest remaining rung. Hays climbs directly below, and at least two Horrors are closing fast.

Battson lowers the rope down the shaft. "Hays, you okay down there?"

"Hurry," the dwarf shouts. "The patients can't wait."

The dwarf rants so loudly that Battson's ears don't register the scraping across the sticky stone floor until a cold hand grabs his leg. He twists around and falls on his ass.

The impact jolts up his spine.

Clutching his ankle is what's left of the Page. Whole chunks of his face are missing, and one torn eyeball hangs from its socket. On his left arm, bones protrude through ripped blankets of flesh.

He tries shoving the hellish creature away, but Cobb lunges and lands shoulder-first on Battson's stomach. He sputters for breath and squeezes Cobb's throat. The Horror squirms forward, oblivious. Can't choke the dead.

The Horror moans, and the stench of spoiled eggs wafts between its broken teeth. Its fingernails dig into Battson's wrists. With a grunt, Battson shoves Cobb backward and wedges a boot onto the Horror's chest. With one powerful thrust, he kicks the foppish Horror down the shaft.

The dwarf below yells first in pain, then terror. Quick as a water moccasin, the rope Battson hasn't yet anchored begins snaking into the shaft.

Chapter Thirty-Seven

Grouchy

HIS SNOWFLAKE. HER BLOOD-RED eyes—lumps of coal
floating in tomato soup—stare at him hungrily. She bends down
to where the fuses intersect on the ground. She cocks her head,
breathes quick, shallow rasps.

Grouchy's match burns down until it scorches his fingers.

He should light the fuse now, but can't. The explosion would
tear her apart, and clearly she's different than the other Horrors. She
hasn't hissed and lunged. She's studying the web of fuses.

Maybe she's getting better.

A thought blossoms in Grouchy's head. Maybe the dandy-ass
Prince wasn't her true love and that's why Snow woke up wrong.
Maybe if she had a kiss from a love that was true, like him, she
would be okay.

One kiss, and he can cure her.

The flame bites his fingers.

"Shit." He drops the match.

Snow extends a hand under the lowest of the fuses and swings her arm in a slow, lazy arc, gradually collecting each fuse in her palm and popping each out of its explosive.

With a flick of her fingers, the fuses fall to the ground.

She steps closer. Viscera and ash coat her yellowed dress. Her comb still protrudes from her singed hair. Dried blood and gristle cover her beautiful face, likewise her chest. All he can think of is vanilla ice cream smothered in raspberry sauce. And, of course, *how the hells is that comb still in her hair?*

His Snowflake smiles, her teeth now stained dirty red. She tilts her chin at him, her head still cocked at that jaunty angle like a scarecrow on a post. With a glance down the spiral passage, she bellows a raspy hiss like a rusty blade drawn across a porous rock.

For a moment, only silence.

From below, a chorus of ghoulish voices hisses in response. She's communicating with them.

Balls.

Still smiling, she turns back to Grouchy and waves a quick wiggle of her fingers now topped with shattered nails.

B-bye.

Grouchy's stomach tightens into a hard shell. He turns and runs, chancing one last look back at his beautiful Snow. She's there, still waving.

No longer smiling.

Chapter Thirty-Eight

Snoozy

AT LAST, A ROPE wiggles blindly down the shaft, almost within grasp. Just three more rungs to go. The rope sways back and forth like a worm on a hook. Snoozy hauls his bulk up another rung and chews, chews, chews.

Two more rungs.

Hays climbs right below him, pursued by two Horrors. Hanging to a rung, Hays kicks at the Horrors and stomps their fingers. Further below, the darkness swells deep and dark as an apple core. The seed. Need. Freed. Snoozy pops his last root into his mouth.

"Almost there?" Hays says, panting.

Before Snoozy can answer, a Horror grabs Hays' ankle. The soldier kicks free, but his face hangs all weary. Snoozy looks up and chews, chews, chews.

One more rung.

But then a mangled Cobb plummets down the shaft. Snoozy raises an arm over his head before Cobb's blood-splattered ass slams into him like a sack of coal.

"Ahh," Snoozy yells.

He grabs the rope, except the rope keeps coming. He falls only a short distance before the rope jerks taut. He gasps with the impact, and the jumble of root flies out of his mouth.

He screams in horror.

His precious root.

Snoozy doesn't even notice frail, mutilated Cobb dangling from his ankle until the ghoulish Page gnaws on the toe of his boot. That snaps him back to reality.

A reality he can't face.

He's dangling from a rope. Over a greedy darkness. An undead human's gnawing on his boot. His roots are all gone. Gobbled by the darkness. By the core. By the dark hunger that threatens to consume him—to end his own hunger. His own desperation. He takes a resolute breath and closes his eyes.

And lets go.

He is ready to return to his roots.

But someone grabs his wrist. His eyes snap open. Hays swings him through the air against the wall. The impact shoves the breath from his body. Below, Cobb swings with him, colliding with the Horror attacking Hays. The two Horrors' heads thud together, and they flail into the darkness with a trailing moan and an irritated hiss.

"Grab on," Hays says. "We ain't out of the sizzle yet."

Two more demented soldiers scurry upward. Hays climbs quickly, much faster than Snoozy. Snoozy was holding Hays back, and the soldier never complained. This realization gives Snoozy a bit of hope. He climbs after Hays.

Hays reaches the rope and shouts upward, "I'm coming up."

"I'm ready," yells Battson.

The apple's core calls to Snoozy from below: *Don't leave me. I have your roots. Be my soil. We can make such beautiful fruit.*

The Horrors are closing in, just five rungs away. Snoozy spits at them, hoping to expel the root taste out of his mouth, to push the voices out of his head. Meanwhile, Hays and the rope rise upward. Snoozy looks alternately up and down, gauging the progress of the Horrors against the rope.

Four rungs away. Hays hoists himself over.

Three rungs away. The rope trails down the shaft, a dull grey snake biting at the dark.

Two rungs away. Snoozy grabs the rope and yells, "Pull."

One rung away. The rope jerks upward. The frayed material digs into Snoozy's blistered palms. The rope slowly ascends, but abruptly stops.

Now it lowers.

His stomach lurching, Snoozy sees that a ghastly soldier has grabbed the bottom end of the rope. The Horror hisses at him, a line of bloody drool dangling from its lower lip. Too much weight. Too much wait. Too many patients.

Snoozy looks down into the darkness, where the apple core whispers.

Don't leave me.

Chapter Thirty-Nine

Grouchy

GROUCHY RUNS BACK TO the vertical shaft, and thoughts boil in his brain. Snow smiled at him. Waved at him. Summoned the other Horrors. What does this mean? He grabs a skull-sized rock in case the pursuing mob overtakes him. His thoughts cease when he hears the soldiers' voices.

"You threw Cobb at us?" Hays says.

"I'm just saying, pinky," Battson says. "Seemed like a good idea at the time. Where's Captain?"

"Cap'n ain't here no more."

Battson doesn't respond. Grouchy finds the two soldiers braced against the floor at the top of the shaft, holding onto a rope suspended below. The area surrounding the shaft is bare aside from blood and debris, offering nothing to grab for support. By leveraging themselves against the floor, they've kept the rope from descending further, but they can't pull it upward. The shaft's sharp lip has frayed the rope, now a raggedy flower blooming from a tired stem.

"The worms are hungry," Snoozy moans below. "The core is whispering"

Across from the soldiers, Grouchy limps to the shaft's edge. Below, Snoozy dangles from the rope, as does a bald soldier Horror. Where the hells is Merry?

"Do I have to do every damn thing myself?" Grouchy lobs the rock down the shaft. It strikes the Horror, who hisses in response and thrashes even more. "Like that, you grisly spud?"

He hurls another rock, which smacks the Horror in the ear. Its head snaps to one side and the Horror plummets below with a ragged hiss. After an abrupt thud, a soft moan emanates from the darkness.

Hays and Battson pull upward as Grouchy limp-runs around the shaft to assist. The rope's fray blossoms wider. With a grunt, he lunges.

The rope snaps.

He snatches it below the break, inhales a thankful breath, and hoists the rope upward.

"One of you damn swobs mind dropping your poker to help me out here?"

Hays scrambles to the edge and yanks Snoozy upward. They collapse in a sweaty, gasping pile. Grouchy pats Snoozy's trembling belly. Snoozy nods and blinks his bloodshot eyes several times.

"Hey," Battson says. "I couldn't help not hearing the impressive explosion. I'm just saying. What happened?"

Grouchy's stomach wobbles. He shakes his head. "No time to explain. Where's Merry?"

Hays clears his throat. "He was up here when the lifts fell."

"Shit-cakes." He imagines Merry falling to his death or worse, being made into a meal. His stomach sours, but he chokes out the words. "Then there were two. Let's go."

They sprint—a pair of dwarfs and a pair of humans—down the northwest passage, and the oncoming horde closes fast. Hays leads the way, carrying a lantern. Grouchy's at the rear, panting and limping. His throat and lungs play host to a swarm of angry bees. What he wouldn't give for some water. And a big damn meal.

At the staging chamber, all four of them pant, ready to collapse. The headless corpses are strewn about the room.

"What happened here?" Hays says, coughing.

"No time to explain," Battson says with a dismissive wave of his hand.

Hays runs for the blood-stained tunnel dug into the caved-in exit. He's halfway into the tunnel when Battson yells, "Wait."

Something hisses, yanks Hays into the tunnel. Battson lunges and pulls him backward. The two soldiers tumble onto the floor. It's then that Grouchy notices the captain's wings pinned to Hays chest.

"Can't go that way," Battson says, gasping.

"It's too narrow anyway." Grouchy points at his generous waist.

"What the hell was that?" Hays says.

Snoozy shines a lantern into the tunnel, then waves. "Hi, Bones."

Hissing and the frantic scrambling of rocks answer him. Grouchy guides Snoozy away from the entrance and pats his belly.

Before turning his back on the tunnel, Grouchy locks eyes with the elder dwarf. Bones' eyes were always so full of energy, but now they're filled past the brim with dark rage. He hates how things ended between him and his elder.

"I'm sorry." Grouchy mouths the words—too little, too late.

"Alrighty then." Hays says. "We make our stand here. Everyone grab a weapon."

"No," Grouchy says. "There's another way. Follow me."

With his lantern dimmed and away from his face, he leads them at a jog into the abandoned northeast passage. There, tears slide down his cheeks. And for once, they are not tears for his Snowflake.

No, these tears belong to Bones, who Grouchy disappointed. To Blushful and Dim and Coughy. And especially to Merry. What he wouldn't give to see that dumb idiotic smile one more time.

Chapter Forty

Merry and Captain Ritchards

WHEN MERRY WAKES IN the all-consuming darkness, his cup runs over with agony. His legs are bags of shredded meat stuffed with shattered glass. Splinters and dust in his lungs provoke coughs that feel like angry fists punching inside his broken chest. He whimpers.

Nearby, something groans, and his blood runs cold.

A human voice speaks, "Hays, is that you? You alright, son?"

"Captain?" Merry coughs. "Oh, good. I thought I might have been dead."

"Merry? How the hell did you get all the way down here?"

He chuckles. "I fell, Captain."

"How bad is it? Are you okay?"

"Judging by the agony, I'd say both my legs are broken." He coughs. "Some ribs, too. Fingers . . ." He reaches into his pocket and grabs his worry stone with twisted fingers. "Can't forget the fingers."

"What happened?"

"The Page tried warning us, but he—" Merry coughs again, and thorny hands clench his insides. "He hit his head on the ceiling. By the time I found him, it was too late. The Horrors swarmed us." His laughter collapses into sobs.

———◆———

CAPTAIN RITCHARDS LIES HALF-BURIED in rubble. His punctured skin is full of cold sand and broken seashells. This must be what it's like to drown, only instead of water he's smothered by rocks, darkness, and dread.

Merry's damp chuckling goes on and on. Ritchards must focus on the dwarf.

"Can you see where we are?" Ritchards says. "Is there a way out?"

Merry sniffles. "Dwarfs can't see in pitch blackness. But I'm guessing we're trapped in the alcove on the bottom level."

"Merry, I have something important to tell you."

"First, I have a question, Captain Ritchards. Do you have anything to eat?"

How can the dwarf think of food at a time like this? "No, I'm sorry. I don't."

Merry laughs. Or cries.

"Listen to me, Merry. Earlier, I was bitten."

"Ah."

"The curse is moving through me. I don't have much time. *You* don't have much time."

"Of course I don't. This is all so darn typical." Merry raises his trembling voice. "Are you happy, darkness? You finally have me." Now he's calm, almost conversational. "Go ahead. Eat me."

"Merry, listen. Come to me. Bash in my skull. It's your only chance. Shit, it's my only chance. Please."

"You know what, Captain?" Merry sighs. "It's not easy smiling all the time."

———◦◆———

MERRY SITS UP ON his elbows, and pain shoots through his pelvis down to the tips of his toes. Tears roll down his cheeks. He collapses and squeezes his worry stone so hard that he's sure juice will come out.

Not too far away, and yet from an impossible distance, the captain murmurs, "You can do it, Merry. Kill me. I don't want to become one of them. Save yourself. Kill me."

"Settle down," he says. "I'm coming."

"Come on, little dwarf. Kill me, dammit. Get your grinning ass over here."

Again Merry's bruised elbows meet the ground, and he hoists himself over a rock. Something pops in his leg, like a bite of celery. He screams. It's easy to imagine that scream echoing throughout every crevice in the mine, his boundless agony disrupting the already weakened shaft and causing more rock to spill downward, crushing his head like a grape. Merry's tears turn to laughter because that scenario would be a small mercy. He laughs not just at himself but at the darkness. With a grunt, he throws his worry stone into the void.

Plink. Plink. It bounces away.

"Dammit, Merry. Focus. What's so funny?"

"I finally won, Captain. I beat the darkness." Now he's cackling—even though each crackle of his voice is a flaming whip snapped against his bloody insides. "It doesn't scare me anymore."

"Merry. Now." Even on the brink of death, Ritchards' voice is still full of authority. "The curse is taking me."

"Okay." If the captain says Merry can do it, it must be so. He pushes. Wooden splinters jab into his back, and his frantic laughter immediately ceases. He grunts with determination. If he can kill the captain, he can dig himself out. It'll take time, but he can do it. And Grouchy and Snoozy will come for him. They'll bring Dr. Killington.

"I hear you, Merry. You're getting closer."

———— ◆ ————

RITCHARDS KEEPS TALKING SO that Merry can find him in the dark—and because Merry needs anger to live through this.

"Get your fat ass over here. You know you want to. What dwarf wouldn't want to bash in a human's head? You won't even need a stepladder this time."

Ritchards is too cold now even to shiver. His bones are ice. His blood is frozen sap.

"Get your fat ass over here."

He's fading. Emptiness tingles behind his eyes.

"Dammit, come on."

Nearby, rocks scramble. Merry whimpers and grunts. He must be almost within reach.

"You're right here, Merry. Good." His speech breaks up as his lungs freeze. "Do it. Find my."

His body goes limp.

"Voice and."

His heartbeat is a sluggish murmur.

"Kill me."

And then, a teasing flash of peace. His veins explode with fire. The emptiness in his belly boils up his throat. Thirst ravages his tongue. Not for water. Not for rum.

For blood.

———— ◆ ————

THE DARKNESS THROBS WITH bad intentions. Merry closes his eyes to it, a pointless gesture. Another scoot. Rest. He clutches his belly, not at all surprised to find a broken rib sticking out of his side. The bone's surprisingly warm.

He reaches out, clutches handfuls of shadow. "Just keep talking, Captain." He finds a fist-sized rock. "Captain?"

But what answers isn't the captain. It's a raspy hiss.

Spittle dots Merry's face. He swings the rock blindly. It hits softness, and something grabs his wrist. Merry jerks backward, the broken bones in his legs grinding together.

He screams.

The captain hisses in response, flailing at the debris. He's digging himself out. Merry drags himself backward—agony dancing feverishly in his bones. Maybe he can call for help. The other soldier, Hays, may well be trying to rescue them.

Dragging himself is too exhausting, so he rolls across the debris instead. His legs snap, crackle, and pop. His broken ribs saw at his flesh. The captain keeps flailing until there's a dreadful silence, punctuated only by panting breaths.

If he can stay quiet enough, perhaps the Horror won't find him. Choking down a cough, Merry extends one hand into the dark, patting every few inches in hopes of finding a weapon.

Debris. Splinters of wood.

Pebbles. Another hand.

Merry jerks away, but something hot and heavy lunges forward. Broken teeth tear into Merry's cheek. A hot tongue laps at the blood spilling out of his face. Suddenly, all his fear and dread funnel into one overpowering sensation: thirst.

"No. Oh, please—"

Chapter Forty-One

Grouchy

"THIS IS A WHOPPING bootful of stupid," Battson says as he peers down the northeast passage's vertical shaft. "I'm just saying."

Two dwarfs, two humans. The last of the Collective and the remains of a platoon. The stifling darkness below huffs and growls, or at least that's what Grouchy imagines. The cool air smells of dust and minerals.

"The damn bear didn't hatch down there," Grouchy says. "It came in from outside. If that big bastard got in, then we can get the hells out."

"Yeah, stump. But we still have to get past the bear."

"I don't like bears." Snoozy fidgets with his beard. "All hollow and wooden. Should we knock first?"

Battson rolls his eyes. "I don't recall our last run-in with Mr. Bear going altogether smoothly."

"Because you didn't follow orders, ass-pit."

"Because I don't take orders from stumps. You want to boss me around, figure out a way to do it while looking me in the eye."

Grouchy already knows a way. It involves slapping Battson's crotch. He's about to enact that plan when Hays intervenes.

"We ain't harvesting a rich bounty of options here. Grouchy, any thoughts on how we deal with the big ball of furry death down there?"

He shrugs. "We're bound to kill it before it kills *all* of us."

Battson smirks. "Great plan, stump."

The thundering footsteps grow closer, and ragged breaths echo down the passage. Grouchy clamps his lantern to his belt and grabs one of the ropes they left behind earlier.

"No time to rappel. We're sliding down. Don't let the rope burn through your hands."

And with that, he swings into the shadows. Even through his gloves, the rope bites into his palms. Still, he's grateful to be off of his busted leg.

Merry.

Dammit.

He misses the prick. That dumbass grin. That big belly.

And Bones.

Seeing Bones felt like a rusty spike twisted in his gut. But what if Bones wasn't outside the mine simply because he couldn't fit through the tunnel? What if he was under orders to guard the exit? Orders from Snow?

Grouchy's mismatched boots clop onto the shaft' bottom. Wincing, he whirls the lantern around. The light snags on a crumpled mass—his boot. He examines the drool-covered hunk of torn leather. Frowning, he kicks off the human boot and slides his own disfigured boot over his swollen foot.

Hays lands next, followed by Battson and Snoozy, whose mouth fidgets constantly, his tongue and teeth as busy as ants. Grouchy is ready to slap him when he hears the growl.

With a deafening roar, the bear charges into the shaft, rears up on its hind legs, and smacks Battson to the ground. Grouchy grins at Battson's wide eyes and twisted mouth, then stabs Honey-Stick into the fur-wrapped storm cloud. Hays swings his sword, too, but the beast pins him to the ground and roars—a noise that threatens to bring down the entire mine.

This won't end well.

A Horror plummets down the shaft with a ragged hiss punctuated by a resolute splat of bone and chunky flesh—hot, wet stuff that splatters onto Grouchy's shins. The bear whines as if stabbed by fire and then charges down the passage.

"Follow the bear," Grouchy yells.

"You want us to follow that?" Battson flails his arms.

"It'll lead us outside, dumb-shit." He turns to Snoozy. "Any more fuses?"

Snoozy stares back blankly, only his teeth moving.

With a grunt, Grouchy rummages through Snoozy's pockets—expecting to find roots but instead finding a clump of fuses. "Get him out of here," he says to the others.

The soldiers pull Snoozy after the bear. Grouchy starts to follow, but something grabs his ankle, knocks him to the ground.

It's the soldier who just fell, now a mess of pulped flesh and shattered bone. It turns its head—bones inside its neck crack—and moans. Grouchy kicks at its face, but it won't let go. Above, the dangling ropes wiggle violently. The rest of the Horrors either learned from this one's mistake or—again—they're following orders. Snow's orders.

He kicks until chunky brains cover his boot. After climbing to his feet, he limps down the passage, stopping only to grab a brick of dinermite.

At the end of the passage, he finds Snoozy and the soldiers

making their way through a collapsed wall at the bottom of the northeast spiral. The wall opens into a cavern lit by pale morning late and filled with a jumble of rocks and boulders.

As Grouchy climbs over the rubble, something catches his eye—a figure lurking in the shadows. He aims his lantern and sword at it, only to find a human-sized skeleton fossilized in the rock.

What the holy hells? It's roughly the size of a short human but has the stubby finger bones of a dwarf. Grouchy runs his fingertips over the skeleton's ribcage. Where did it come from?

Footsteps and hisses echo behind him. He scrambles over gravel and rock until, miraculously, fresh air blows against his face. The cavern opens at the other side of the mountain onto a rugged cliff overlooking the Slithering River.

Above, moody clouds obscure most of a dark blue sky. It's morning, early enough that the full moon still nudges at the clouds. Hays, Battson, and Snoozy are already climbing down the cliff.

Grouchy stuffs a fuse into the explosives and lights it. Sparks crackle and consume the length of cotton.

"Down, dammit," he yells.

He throws the dinermite back into the cavern and runs. The sound of the explosion prefaces a wave of debris. The ground lurches beneath his feet, and rock fragments smack into his back. The force launches him from the cliff into the open air. He lands head-first into Slithering River's icy-cold embrace. After that, he does what any dwarf would do in the same situation.

He sinks.

Chapter Forty-Two

Grouchy

GROUCHY GRASPS AT THE water, which unravels into shreds between his fingers and instantly weaves into a liquid blanket—smothering him. His soaked clothes pull him deeper into the river. He yells an angry swarm of bubbles.

His lungs are on the verge of bursting when a hand grabs his beard and pulls him to the surface. He swallows a deep breath of chilled air, then another.

Still holding Grouchy's beard, Battson swims the dwarf to shore with an irritating grace.

Abrasive rocks and withered reeds make an uninviting mess of the shore. Trees line this side of the river, and their roots snake out between mud and rock. Grouchy holds on to a root, coughing out water. Debris from the cliff sprinkles the river's surface.

"Over here, pinky," Battson yells to Hays, who's further downstream.

Hays offers a tired wave. Coughing, he wades toward them. Where's Snoozy?

"I didn't think we'd make it out of there," Battson says. "The sky's never looked so good."

Grouchy looks at the sinister clouds lurking above. "Where's Snoozy?"

"Can he swim?" Hays yells.

Grouchy grunts. "There's a reason dwarfs are shaped like stones—because we tend to sink."

"There." Hays points downstream at Snoozy, floating face-down in the water.

"Dammit."

Hays tosses his boots on shore, throws himself into the water, and swims perpendicular to the river's shoving current.

Soon, Grouchy and Battson help Hays haul Snoozy onto shore, a chore that leaves all of them caked with mud. Grouchy puts an ear to his friend's chest and finds a sluggish heartbeat. He puts a hand over Snoozy's mouth.

"Shit. He's not breathing."

"Hang on." Hays pinches Snoozy's nose and blows into his mouth. Coughs. Blows again.

Battson grimaces. "That's disgusting, pinky."

"Shut up," Grouchy says.

Hays blows again, and this time Snoozy chokes and hurls water. Happily, Grouchy sees that some of it splatters onto Battson's cheek.

"You okay?" Grouchy pats Snoozy's belly.

Snoozy nods feebly.

"We made it out, stump," Battson says. "Now where the hell are we?"

"Must be the far side of the mountain," Grouchy says. "Our raft isn't too far from here."

"Huh," Snoozy says between coughs. Still on his back, he

points upward at a blackened stain burnt into the cliff. "Lightning bolt."

Grouchy stares upward. "I'll be cored."

A blackened blemish scars the cliff where lightning struck it last summer—the morning Snow bit the apple.

---•◆•---

THAT MORNING CAME FAR too fast. Grouchy woke at the foot of the spiral staircase from a dreamless sleep. The taste of stale apple whiskey filled his mouth. His stomach was sour, his blood cloudy with mud. Bones stood over him with a knowing smile.

"Planning on joining us today?"

"Balls. I suppose."

Snow, of course, was nowhere in sight. The loft door was shut.

He would have much preferred to stay there with Snow, but couldn't recall what had happened yesternight. Had he kissed her or simply passed out? Or had he kissed her only to have her push him away in revulsion, knocking him down the stairs? He wanted to go to her to clear up any confusion, but no, it was better to sweat out his poison in the mine and give her time to recover.

They would talk that night, he decided. He would explain his true feelings for her—for better or worse. He couldn't hide his love inside his belly anymore.

Choking back vomit, Grouchy staggered out the door and jogged after his fellow dwarfs.

Though the sky was cloudy, only the lightest of rains fell as the Collective prepared to enter the mine. Bones reached into his pocket and handed something to Snoozy, who popped it into his mouth, chewed, sighed.

"Didn't think it was going to rain today," Blushful said.

Dim nodded knowingly and squinted at the sky.

Coughy shivered. "I hope I don't catch a chill."

Merry said, "Should we go back and leave a note for Snow to bring in the laundry?"

But from down the path sounded a cacophony of panicked squirrels, raccoons, and birds. The clouds overhead darkened and churned ominously.

"What is that ruckus?" Merry said.

Dim shook his head, brow furrowed.

"Snow," Grouchy yelled.

They sprinted back to the cottage, Grouchy and Dim at the lead. When he flung open the front door, he found Snow collapsed on the floor. Over her stood an old hag clutching a shiny apple, one solitary bite blemishing its red skin. The witch's shriveled skin was as bumpy and thick as oatmeal, yet her eyes shone brightly. Grouchy lunged at her, but he slipped on a puddle. His back slammed against the wooden floor. His pickled head reeled. The hag threw a chair at the other dwarfs and ran out the back door. Roaring, Grouchy pursued her, his mining pickax clutched in his hands.

The dwarfs chased her through the forest and up the mountain. For such an old hag, she moved quickly. Finally, at the top of a steep cliff, she pulled out a crooked stick—a wand, Bones would later tell them. She smiled, her lips contorting into a vicious slash over her chin.

"Little fools," she said. "My cursed apple has put Snow under a terrible spell—a living nightmare—and only a kiss from her true love can awaken her." She laughed, a noise like roots being torn from soil.

Blood boiling in his belly, Grouchy charged just as a bolt of lightning struck the cliff. Screaming, the hag toppled into the canyon. He scrambled to the edge, looked below, and saw only a pile of blood-splattered rubble at the river's edge. No way could she have survived.

Bones patted Grouchy's sour belly. Grouchy cursed and kicked the poisoned apple over the cliff's edge.

If only he'd stayed behind that day to proclaim his love to his Snowflake, he could have stopped the hag. He could have proven his love for her.

———————•◆•———————

"WHAT?" BATTSON SAYS NOW. "What lightning bolt?"

As if in response to the soldier, a bolt of lightning flashes in the sky. Rain drizzles downward.

"Was a gruesome hag gave Snow the apple," Grouchy says. "Worked for Queen Adara, we reckon. We chased the old bitch into the woods, cornered her on that cliff. She held up a wand, but before she could use it, lightning struck. She fell down here. Bet that same lightning bolt opened the mine and let the bear inside."

Snoozy arches an eyebrow. "Beer inside?"

"Bear." Grouchy shakes his head. "You know—the big furry that attacked us?"

Snoozy's forehead wrinkles. "That was a bear? Weird."

"Why the hell," Battson says, "would your Snow take an apple from a strange old hag? Was she slight in the head?"

Grouchy stands and clenches his fists.

Battson gives him a knowing smirk.

Hays puts a hand on Grouchy's shoulder. "Those Horrors can still backtrack out the mine's front entrance, right?"

Grouchy gives Battson the stink eye. "It'll take the Horrors awhile to get 'round the mountain. We'll make quicker time to Abundance and Dr. Killington in the raft."

"What good is he to us now?" Battson cocks his head. "Your plan went all to shit. We failed to capture the Horrors."

214 | ROB E. BOLEY

After seeing the thirst in Snow's eyes back in the mine, Grouchy suspects that she has plans to visit Abundance and drink deeply of the humans there. Getting there ahead of her is the only chance he'll have to cure her.

"Maybe he'll have some ideas on how to stop her," he says. "Maybe we can rally some of the townspeople to help. You have a better idea?"

No, Battson doesn't.

Ducking in and out of thickets and rocky outcroppings, the dwarfs lead Battson and Hays along Slithering River. The humans have hells' time keeping up because their added height provides extra obstacles. Grouchy gathers berries as he walks, stashing some into a bag and stuffing more into his face. Rain turns the dirt to mud.

"I'm just saying," Battson says. "How can something with such little legs move so fast?"

"Come on, swobs," Grouchy says around a mouthful of berries. "I'd like to reach the fumping village by midday if you gangly darlings are able."

When they reach the raft, Grouchy takes a deep breath of fresh air spiced with rain and dead leaves. The river murmurs calmly now that they've left the shadow of the mountain. Bugs pepper the river's surface, flying to and fro. The humans swat at the pests.

Since Bones usually traveled alone to Abundance, the raft has only two oars. They take turns rowing. Grouchy passes around his bag of berries. The humans partake, but Snoozy declines. Dwarfs never decline food.

The raft glides around a bend, and Grouchy's jaw drops open. By the shore, a naked human woman kneels in the water.

She's older than Snow, yet her body is a miraculous sculpture of all the right curves. Her blond hair hangs just past her shoulders, and her skin is slightly sunburnt, adding depth to her unusual beauty. She's on her knees, the river nipping at her thighs. Head bowed, she whispers at the water—possibly praying? She kisses the river's surface.

"Well," Battson says, "looks like things are finally looking up."

Chapter Forty-Three

Prince Mikael

THE PRINCE IS DEAD.

He spills, slow as a handful of feathers, toward a pinprick of light glowing in the distance. The light doesn't burn. It ripples.

Except dusty air rushes into his lungs. Rusty teeth bite into his soul, yanking him out of the darkness, away from the light.

Not far away, lightning strikes.

Prince Mikael wakes in a dimly-lit cave stinking of blood and mineral. His mouth tastes like rotten fish, and he can't seem to find his honey-gum. Snow leans over him in the dark, her hands on his sculpted chest burning almost painfully hot, yet nourishing. It almost feels like her hands work inside him, massaging his soul, urging him back to life. Except she's not giving him life. No. No, she's taking away death. Her fingertips throb and wiggle, working the death from his bones the way his chamber maidens would work soreness from his muscles.

Snow is an angel, a savior. He smiles, reassured that—once again—his intuitions proved superior.

From the first moment he saw her, he knew that Snow was special—that she was more than her lowly station in life. He was at the Eastern Kingdom's Chamber House for a summit about the Dwarf Situation. Dwarfs were never a problem or a crisis. Always a situation. The summit was in recess, as it would be for most of the day, so he and a duke explored the Bella Gardens surrounding the Chamber House. They smoked petalweed and laughed while his Page looked on disapprovingly.

Soon, the duke collapsed on the ground, fondling an assortment of orchids. Mikael popped a fresh piece of honey-gum into his mouth and wandered deeper into the gardens, drawn by the most peculiar song. Soon he came to a clearing far off the path. There, a flock of mismatched birds—finches, parakeets, swans, and ducks—twittered a glorious symphony.

The birds surrounded a young woman with raven hair and blood-red lips. Her skin was as pale and unblemished as ivory. She sang along with the birds with a surprisingly throaty voice for one so young:

> Jack took the maiden Jill to the top of the hill
> And reached under her resplendent chemise.
> Jill would have fought back but Jack used such skill
> On every part of her he expertly seized.
> Jack then sat himself on the edge of the well
> And Jill sat upon on overturned bucket.
> Jill rubbed Jack's crown which took to swell
> And so she decided to fump it.

He laughed heartily, and the birds scattered. He locked eyes with that coarse maiden. Approaching, he bowed and offered his pipe. She giggled and plucked the pipe from his hand. She inhaled, blinked longingly, and exhaled several smoke rings. A small bluebird flew in and out of the rings until the smoke dispersed.

She said her name was Snow. From that moment on, the world was a little bit brighter and deeper.

Except now the world is flatter, duller.

In stark contrast, he has never felt so strong. It's as if Snow is somehow pulling out of him any weakness, any potential at illness. Energy throbs between his bones, but his vision has gone flat like a painting.

He touches his handsome face and finds that one of his eye sockets is clotted and sticky. He's lost an eye. One of his beautiful, perfect eyes. Impossible. He's the Prince.

Above, Snow's ragged breath intensifies. He sits up and squints at her face. Her torn lips. Her blood-stained chin. Oh, no. This won't do at all.

"Oh, my dearest love, what—"

Before he can finish, Snow darts forward and kisses him full on the mouth. Her breath tastes of sour milk and coppery blood. She pushes against him and licks at his teeth. He struggles against her, tries turning his head. Their teeth clink together. Her nails sink into his neck, and his jaw jerks open. She sucks at his tongue, then bites down. He tastes his own royal blood spilling from his severed tongue.

With that one wicked kiss, fire erupts in his veins.

Long live the Prince.

Chapter Forty-Four

Grouchy

GROUCHY KNOWS LITTLE OF human social etiquette. And really, he can't imagine there's a standard polite way for young men to greet a naked woman standing in a river. Still, Battson's approach leaves something to be desired.

"Ma'am," Battson booms. "Pardon our intrusion, but we simply must insist that you come with us. Terrible creatures are in the vicinity, and your safety is in jeopardy. But have no fear. As a trained soldier, I will make it my formal duty to protect you from harm's way. As will my fellow soldier-in-training and our dwarf servants."

"Servants, my gelatinous ass," Grouchy says.

"Ignore him," Hays says to Grouchy. "If you can."

Grouchy expects the woman to cover herself in surprise, but instead she rises, hands at her side, head cocked, appraising the raft. Rain drips down her bare skin. Eventually, Battson's head bows in embarrassment, which seems to trigger something in her. She covers her private bits and hurries out of the water. After she slips into a simple white dress hanging from a nearby bush, she returns to shore, her arms crossed over her chest. She shivers.

The two soldiers stare at her, entranced, as Grouchy paddles the raft to shore. Her delicate nose slopes over full lips and a pointed chin. Her slightly freckled face and arms flush pink from the sun. Her jewel-like beauty contrasts with her tangled hair, bruised knees, and fierce eyes.

Hays, stepping on shore, clears his throat. "Apologies, ma'am. We're traveling to a village called Abundance. Are you from there?"

She shakes her head. "I'm from Platessa. My husband and I, we were traveling to visit family. We set up camp yestereve, but then a—a bear attacked us."

A tear spills from her eye. Hays fumbles for a handkerchief, but Battson beats him to it.

She takes the handkerchief, dabs tears and rain from her eyes. "My husband, he pushed me away. Told me to run as fast and as far as I could while he fought off the bear. I ran into the dark. So dark. All I could hear was screaming—horrible screaming."

Battson pats her shoulder. "I'm Battson and this is Hays. We are soldiers from the Western Kingdom, sent here by Queen Theabella to escort our prince. Hays is new to this, but I am a seasoned soldier. I'd be happy to escort you to Abundance. There, we can organize a search party for your husband. But we must go now. There is little time to waste."

Hays grits his teeth. Clearly Grouchy is not the only one irritated by Battson.

Grouchy waves. "And I'm Grouchy. This is Snoozy."

"A pleasure to meet you." She offers a trembling smile. "*All* of you. My name is Fairess. Thank you for helping me. I didn't know what I was going to do. It's such a strange forest. I heard no other animals last night, and no birds singing this morning. Isn't that strange?"

The clouds above sprinkle rain.

"The birds took their songs away when our other lady friend started eating everyone," Snoozy says.

"Snoozy," Grouchy says.

Hays clears his throat again. "Yes, ma'am. The monsters we mentioned earlier put a streak of fear into all the local critters."

"Monsters?"

"We'll explain soon enough," Battson says. "But we should be going."

She nods. "Can I bring a dog? We found each other yesternight. She seemed almost as frightened as I was."

"Yanky," Hays says to himself. Then he yells, "Yanky. Where are you, girl?"

The bushes nearby rustle, and then Yanky leaps into sight, wagging her tail. She knocks Hays over and licks his face.

"Disgusting," Battson says under his breath.

Hays scratches behind Yanky's ears. "You had me as scared as a skunk in a diaper."

"Fumping wonderful," Grouchy says. "Can we go now?"

By the time everyone is on the raft, the rain intensifies to a steady tapping. Trees usher the raft downstream, their bare limbs offering little shelter from the raindrops. Mosquitoes and other bugs swarm the river's surface, biting at the travelers whenever possible. The soldiers tell Fairess about the Horrors. Battson, of course, casts himself as the hero. She stares back, wide-eyed, and nods along.

Eventually, they settle into the raft and let the river push them downstream. Snoozy keeps his eyes closed and rocks back and forth. Fairess starts humming a simple melody. Hays molds a lump of clay into a leafless tree.

Grouchy lights his pipe and puffs quietly. The smoke tastes

strong and sweet. He sighs, sends a smoky worm wiggling behind the raft.

He closes his eyes and tries to remember the last moment he was able to enjoy a smoke without Horrors pounding on doors or digging through rocks to murder him. It was two nights ago, his last alone time with Bones.

————◆————

GROUCHY SMOKED HIS PIPE while Bones stared at the full moon. The elder dwarf fidgeted with his beard, as if nervous—or expectant. Overhead, bats flew noiselessly in erratic patterns, snatching bugs out of the air.

"Let's talk about your anger," Bones said finally.

"Ah. A new subject."

"You hold onto your hate, Grouchy, but I fear it will serve you ill in the days ahead."

"I don't hold it. I use it, same as I would use a pickaxe or shovel."

"I fear that it uses you."

Grouchy laughed a cloud of smoke. "You fear too much. If you want to worry about someone, worry about Merry."

"We're talking about you. When someone wrongs you, it is right to be angry. The anger can nudge you to make things right. But if you hang on to that anger, it keeps you from healing. There is much power in forgiveness."

"You would have me forgive the swobs for all that they've done to us?"

"To us, or to you?"

Grouchy puffed his pipe and rolled his eyes. "If there's a point here, do get to it."

Bones stared at him, furrowed his brow. "Grouchy, you have

a deep stomach—deeper than most—and that's what makes you special. Yet you stuff your belly full of anger and cling to that suffering because it makes you feel better than your brothers to have suffered more. Hurt more. Endured more. You think that makes you special—that it makes you stronger—but really it makes you weaker. It makes you a victim. And until you grow up and let go of that anger and learn to forgive, you'll only be a victim."

———— ◆ ————

TWITTERING NOTES SNAP GROUCHY out of his thoughts.

His eyes pop open. Have the birds returned?

No, it's Snoozy. He holds his miraculously unharmed flute to his lips and blows the notes of a carefree little ditty that clashes entirely with present circumstances. No one complains. In fact, Hays smiles.

The young captain swats at a bug. "Is this normal for y'all here in the East? To have so many bugs, even when it rains?"

Grouchy grunts. "No birds—no predators to eat the bugs. And this ain't nothing. You should see the bugs in the Dwarflands."

Snoozy continues his melody, which brings to mind flapping wings, trickling raindrops, and galloping squirrels. Soon, everyone sways or pats with the music. Fairess and Battson hum along. They exchange a look.

"No way," Battson says, pointing at Snoozy. "Can't be. Are you? You are. You're the Little Wind, aren't you?"

Snoozy nods.

"I saw you play years ago," Fairess says.

Battson nods. "My father took me to see you play at the Cope Land Amphitheater in Carpaldal. You were amazing. I begged him to buy me a flute afterward. I never played it ended up trading it to my brother Stuglas for fireworks." He turns to Fairess. "Where did you see him play?"

She shrugs. "At the garden amphitheater."

"Really?" Battson cocks his head. "I didn't know the Eastern Kingdom had an amphitheater."

She waves a dismissive hand. "I was so young."

All the while, Grouchy just stares. "Holy tit-milk. What the hells are you talking about?"

"You don't know who this is?" Battson says. "He's probably the most famous dwarf musician ever."

Grouchy snorts. "Little Wind?"

"It was my stage name." Snoozy stares down at his flute as he talks, his fingers still working the holes. "I toured the three kingdoms, played for kings and queens. The crowds. The never-ending roads. The brilliant scenery. The bountiful food. All the drink and smoke I wanted."

"Is it true you puked on King Roderique?" Battson says.

Snoozy nods. "I did far worse than that. I was banned from the Ascendio Kingdom. I set fire to the Western Kingdom's amphitheater. It didn't take me long to ruin everything I'd achieved. And so, here I am."

"Balls." Grouchy shakes his head. "You think you know somebody."

Chapter Forty-Five

Queen Adara

THE RAFT DRIFTS DOWNSTREAM. In contrast to the river's leisurely pace, Adara's heart pounds a jagged rhythm. She sits with two strapping soldiers and two stinky dwarfs, bound for a village named Abundance. Well-trained at hiding her emotions from her life as a princess and then a queen, she conceals her fear of the watery depths. She can't swim and has feared the water since her youth.

The boy soldier Battson keeps talking to her. She tries to focus on his words, but the bear's memory of the boy nudges her mind. Once she almost claws him across the face. Still, the handsome boy could prove useful.

Other animalistic urges linger in Adara's mind, echoes of her recent victims. She longs to swallow the plentiful bugs swarming the water—to swoop down like a bat and skim a drop of water from the water's surface. Indeed, the river's trickling rhythm stirs in her the need to construct a damn. Her teeth ache to gnaw on wood. She laughs at herself, and Battson seems pleased. He must have just said something he thought to be witty.

She can't believe that no one recognizes her. Granted, she isn't wearing her royal attire. Her face is unpainted and tanned by the sun. Her hair is wild, unbrushed. She's not herself and she hasn't been for quite a while.

Not since she transformed herself into that old hag last summer, gave that damned apple to Snow, and fell off the cliff.

———————◆————————

SHE KNEW SOMETHING HAD gone wrong as soon as Snow bit the apple. Adara's vision wobbled, and pain stabbed into her brain. Panic needled at her heart. It didn't make sense. The apple's curse was only supposed to affect Snow. Before she could ponder this further, those miserable stumps arrived and chased her through the woods. She led them up a steep cliff, where she stood over them in triumph.

Except a bolt of lightning ruined what should have been her moment of victory. She tumbled below into the unforgiving river's embrace.

She woke a changed woman. The fall broke her body, but the apple had somehow crippled her magical powers. She couldn't even cast a simple flame enchantment to cook her dinners. Thankfully, she could still command the lesser creatures of the forest. She also found a new use for them.

Inexplicably, she could now absorb the life force from animals. By simply placing her palms upon the creatures, she could drain their life—and their memories—into herself.

She used this new power to heal herself over the course of many moons. In the process, she forged a connection with the forest. Aside from some choice furs, she stopped wearing clothing, preferring instead the freedom of nakedness. There amongst the creatures and trees, she was free of gossip, betrayal, politics, etiquette, and all the blankets of humanity that smothered her in her former life. Alas, that freedom was not meant to last.

Yestermorn, shortly after sunrise, agony pierced her skull. In the same instant, all the birds in the forest took flight into the darkening sky. She commanded them to return, but they ignored her.

They. Ignored. *Her.*

Since that moment, a fracture has festered in her mind. She spent all of yesterday preparing, at last, to leave the forest. She tore down her primitive shelter and cleaned her simple white dress. Her heart throbbed with dread.

Last night was the first time she really missed her spells. It was also the first time she felt truly afraid.

She couldn't sleep. It was as if whatever path inside her skull led from wakefulness to dreaming had been destroyed. Whenever she tried to sleep, she saw only bright red flashes of anger, black bruises of pain, and white patches of thirst. Snow. These visions kept her stuck awake like a bug trapped in a web.

Late in the night, the dog, Yanky, found her. They huddled together under the stars. When the beast finally slept, she envied its snoring.

Moments ago, Queen Adara stood with her new canine companion on the banks of the Slithering River. She stared gratefully at the rising sun, even if it was muted by clouds. The dog barked.

A mighty bear huffed and splashed downstream. She commanded the dog away, then stripped and entered the river. She disliked the water, but she dreaded the evil lurking around her even more. The bear charged toward her. The river, shockingly cold, jarred her ankle bones.

"Stop," she said to the bear.

It kept coming.

"Stop," she yelled.

This time it halted directly in front of her.

Teeth chattering from the cold, she placed her hands on the bear's head. He sat with a mighty splash, furry rump smacking the water. He stank of wet fur. Like syrup pouring out of a bottle, the bear's life force trickled into her. She'd never consumed an animal so large.

His memories burst behind her eyes. She saw the bear confront the same mean-eyed dwarf who had chased her up the cliff after Snow bit the apple. Only this time a handsome soldier of the Western Kingdom accompanied the dwarf. The bear chased them and clawed the dwarf's ankle. Later, more dwarfs and soldiers arrived, pursued by an unnatural evil. The bear felt fear at its most primal. Terror.

She'd experienced that same fear all night.

As the bear had collapsed into a puddle of goo and bone, the last of Adara's wounds faded, leaving her as strong as she was before falling off the cliff, if not stronger. She knelt in the water and stared at her reflection for the first time in many moons. She was still beautiful, but her beauty was not perfect. It was more primal. Before, her beauty had been flat, like a painted portrait. But now it had texture and depth. Her time in the wilderness, sleeping under the stars with only animals for company, had changed her inside and out. How many beavers, bats, squirrels, and other creatures had she absorbed? How much of their essence still flickered inside her skull?

Her reflection smiled at her. Oh, how she missed her Mirror. How she craved its attentions.

"Tell me," she said. "Tell me who is the fairest of them all."

Of course, the river did not answer. She kissed her reflection. It did not kiss her back.

And then the raft appeared. And on it, two soldiers and two dwarfs.

Magic is a naughty beast.

If only she had waited a few extra moments to absorb the bear, she could have commanded it to kill them all. If she still had the ability to cast spells, she could have conjured some offense against them—drowned them with an angry wave or attacked them with an enchanted paddle.

Not to worry, though. She'll take care of them in due time.

———— • ♦ ————

SOON THE RAFT THUMPS against a wooden dock, knocking Adara from her thoughts.

The sun perches overhead in a nest of clouds. Rain drizzles lazily. They follow a trail leading to a precipice overlooking the town.

The buildings stand one or two stories tall, jammed shoulder to shoulder like commoners in a crowded room. Other than abandoned wagons, the muddy streets are empty. Crimson flags hang heavy with rain. A Hopish church sits in the middle of town, its spire pointing upward at the sky. It reminds Adara of her father, King Roderique of the Ascendio Kingdom. She shivers.

Yanky whimpers and paws at the ground.

Grouchy spits. "We finally made it. Our journey is almost over." The little runt says this like he's trying to believe it.

"Do we need to go there?" the stump Snoozy says.

"What?" Grouchy says.

"Why is this our responsibility? We didn't create the curse. This is a human problem now. Let them deal with it."

Adara smiles to herself. As if a dwarf could create or destroy a curse this mighty.

The nasty Grouchy pats Snoozy's belly. "What about Bones? And Snow? And Dim? Those are our damn friends, Snooze."

"What does this place have to offer us? We don't belong here."

"We go to Killington's, see what he can do."

"If nothing else," Hays says, "the doctor will have herbs and medicines to treat our wounds."

"Herbs?" Snoozy's eyes flash. "Let's go, then."

"Where are all the people?" Hays says.

Battson shrugs. "Maybe it's lunch. Do you of the Eastern Kingdom retire for lunch?"

Adara nods. "Yes. But still, we should see some indication of life."

No one responds as they digest the implication of her words. In the absence of life, there is death. Death in Abundance.

Chapter Forty-Six

Grouchy

THE LITTLE GROUP OF survivors files through Abundance's narrow, muddy, deserted streets. The village smells of apple pie, caramel, and beer. Trash and debris litter the streets. Grouchy sees more than a few children's toys—carved figurines and cloth dolls of heroic princes, vicious wolves, fair maidens, and, of course, a crude likeness of Queen Adara herself. He steps on a Queen doll and grinds the nasty bitch into the mud. Just like on the river, an unusual number of flies, gnats, and bees buzz here and there.

Grouchy frowns at the always-visible church spire. Swobs. What dipshits want to spend eternity floating in the clouds? And if heaven's in the sky, why antagonize it by poking it with churches? Fumping swobs.

Dwarfs are not usually outside at this time of day, but the clouds make the sunshine easier to tolerate. Grimly, he remembers the Horrors' dilated eyes. The clouds will benefit them, too.

"Let's stick to the alleys," Battson says. "The stumps might attract the wrong kind of attention."

"Agreed." Hays shoots Battson a look. "Looks like there's been a festival. Maybe everyone is sleeping off a bellyful of wicked water."

"Wish I was," Snoozy says as he ducks into the alley.

Drenched sheets and laundry hang from ropes strung across the alley, which stinks of piss and rotten food. Rain patters patiently. Yanky whines constantly, her nose to the ground and her eyes to the sky. Even in the alley, the subtle stench of sticky apple persists. The stink brings to mind the apple that started this curse. He pictures it now, clutched in that nasty hag's clawlike hand.

Up ahead, the woman Fairess says nothing, but simply watches the sky. Grouchy doesn't know what to make of her, except that her nose reminds him of his Snowflake's—both as round and delicate as sugardrops.

Grouchy stays at the rear of the group, where he mutters obscenities under his breath and drags his battered, bitten, twisted leg through the mud. A cloud brews in his belly far darker than any in the sky. That cowpoker Hays finds his long-lost doggy, Battson gets to drool all over a damsel in distress, and even fumping Snoozy gets to be famous. And what does he get? A fumping limp.

Battson's dim shadow falls over Grouchy. It's the first moment the boy has let Fairess get out of arm's reach since they found her in the river.

"She's a little old for you, ain't she, swob?" Grouchy points at Fairess, whose curved buttocks nudge hypnotically against her simple dress.

"Is age all that important?" Battson says. "How young was that Snow of yours, anyhow?"

"Shut up."

They walk in silence for a few moments, past more deserted buildings. Grouchy can tell Battson's slowing his steps to match

Grouchy's pace.

The boy fidgets with the handle of his sword. "I wanted to, uh, thank you for saving me back there."

Grouchy sighs. "Which time?"

"Whatever."

They plod onward. Raindrops and footsteps. Pain nips at Grouchy's knee, the hurt somehow strengthened by the silence.

"I pulled you out of the water, you know," Battson says at last. "You were drowning."

"Uh-huh."

"You could thank me, too." Battson grins. "I'm just saying. I was damn heroic."

To Grouchy's surprise, he doesn't want to punch the smile off of Battson's face. His mind fumbles, trying to reconcile his hatred for humans with his growing tolerance for this annoying soldier. Loving Snow is one thing, but buddying up with a human soldier?

"If someone had told me yesterday," Grouchy says, "that I'd save a swob soldier's life and he'd save mine, I'd have laughed my shaggy ass off."

"Yeah." Battson nods. "But what happens when this is all over?"

Grouchy shrugs. "Hopefully we're about to find out."

Hays leads them to a two-story structure. A sign hangs above the back door bearing two red flowers—the symbol for medical care. It reads:

DOCTOR KILLINGTON
LEAVE YOUR AXE AT THE DOOR
LEAVE YOUR ACHES INSIDE

The doctor's office snuggles between a post office and a barbershop. Clumps of hair—brown, black, and white—litter the damp ground. Across the alley stands a pub called the Abominable Axe. Battson nudges past Hays to open the door for Fairess.

"Shall we?" he says.

After she steps inside, Battson follows and lets the door slam in Grouchy's face. Hays shakes his head and holds the door open for the dwarfs and the dog.

The first floor of Killington's office holds a dense assortment of worn-out chairs, a desk cluttered with parchments and wicked-looking tools, and shelves jammed with jars of herbs and specimens. A marked-up skeleton hung from the ceiling lurks in one corner. The apple scent lingers in the air. Grouchy picks up a golden ball resting next to three broken iron bands stained with either rust or blood. The ball's light weight surprises him. He stares at the round orb and thinks again of that wicked apple and how it fell out of the hag's hand before she fell off the cliff. It landed with the bitten side up, exposing the spot where Snow's precious teeth tore into its crisp flesh. Damn that hag. Damn that queen.

Nearby, Fairess runs a finger down a flecked mirror and frowns. Yanky shakes herself off, spraying the dwarfs.

"Shit-cakes." Grouchy wipes his face.

"Suppose the skeleton is real?" Snoozy says, his eyes wide.

"Probably a former patient." Grouchy plucks the skeleton's ribs and notices a rectangular indentation in the ceiling about the width and length of a human coffin. He points upward. "I think that's a trapdoor."

Hays pushes a chair underneath. "Let's take a look."

Battson smirks. "Who put you in charge, pinky?"

"Cap'n did." Hays steps on the chair.

Heh. Clearly, Battson isn't shitting daisies over Hays' promotion. Well, good.

The trapdoor has no handle, so Grouchy hands Hays a small

dagger. After some prying, the trapdoor creaks downward to reveal a set of built-in folding stairs. The soldiers unfold the rickety, narrow staircase to the floor and then climb upward. When they disappear from sight, no one speaks. Even Yanky stops whining.

Dread swirls in Grouchy's belly. The muscles in his back tighten. The apple nags at his mind.

Finally, Hays' head appears in the opening. Grouchy sighs. His back relaxes, and his belly expands.

Hays motions them upward.

The staircase leads to an open loft crowded with a dozen wooden beds. A busted old sign leans against one wall, reading: *MILLGUD BEDS.* At the front, a window overlooks the street below. At the rear is a closed door. Above, the ceiling slopes upward from the two side walls, meeting at a point directly underneath the roof's peak. There, rain nervously taps.

Yanky sniffs at the closed door and tucks her tail between her legs.

Grouchy limps to the door and signals for Hays to kick it in so that he and Battson can charge inside. He pulls out Honey-Stick, testing its heft. He nods at Fairess, watching from across the room. Where the hells is Snoozy?

Hays kicks open the door with a loud thump.

Grouchy charges into a windowless room lined with shelves. A girl emerges from behind two massive trunks, clutching a simple bow with an arrow nocked at the ready.

She fires. Her arrow whizzes over Grouchy's head. From behind him, something roars. He turns in time to see an immense man step from behind the door. The giant shoves him to the floor with an open palm the size of Grouchy's face.

Grouchy slams onto the wood floor with a grunt. Honey-stick clatters next to him. The fur-clad giant standing over him furrows his brow. A mop of dark brown hair tops his head, draping on either side of a square jaw and bushy mustache.

Hays and Battson tackle the man, who stands a full head taller than either soldier. Though a bloodstained bandage covers his forearm, he fights with the strength of a bear. He wraps a beefy forearm around Battson's throat and plants an enormous boot onto Hay's chest. Battson gasps for breath. Hays sprawls on the floor.

Yanky lunges forward and clamps her teeth around the giant's leg. The girl aims her bow at the dog.

Hays shouts, "No," then, "Yanky, off."

"Keep your voice down, you fool," the giant says.

Hays pats the giant's leg. "We don't mean no harm. We're here to see the doctor."

"Do you have an appointment?" says a woman's voice. It belongs to an older woman now standing in the doorway with none other than Dr. Killington. A waterfall of silvery hair spills down either side of her face. Her mouth is slightly sunken, and her nose comes to a prominent point. Wonderfully deep wrinkles highlight her face, indicating she's one who has laughed a great deal. She must be Killington's wife.

The doctor pats her hand. "Not now, Margie." He's a slight man with skeletal fingers, caterpillar eyebrows, and a sprinkling of teeth.

"Daddy?" the girl with the bow asks. She stares at Hays' dog with wide eyes. Her hands tremble. A messy triple ponytail barely contains her long brown hair.

The giant nods. "It's okay, Loxy."

The young girl lowers her bow.

"If you know what's good for you," the giant says, "you'll leave now."

Loxy. The name tickles Grouchy's memories. As he picks himself and his sword up off the floor, he notices the giant's split

ear, like the forked tongue of a snake—like Devere from his
Snowflake's story, the spud-ass who left her to die in the woods.
That means the girl must be Lox, Snow's best friend.

"Balls," Grouchy says. "You're Devere and Lox."

"How do you know our names?" The giant takes a step back
and squints at Grouchy. Before Grouchy can answer, Devere focuses
over Grouchy's shoulder and falls to one knee. "My Queen."

Grouchy turns around and sees only Fairess.

"Keep back," Fairess warns.

Grouchy stares at her and tries to jam this earthy woman's
image into the frame of the awful Queen stored in his mind's eye.
Where's the makeup? Where's the elaborate hair piled atop her
head? She stares back at him, her eyes defiant and cold.

His stomach boils over into a roar—the warrior yell that his
father for so long tried to beat out of him.

"Waarrrrghh!" He lifts Honey-Stick, lunges toward her.

She raises her arms, extends herself to her full height, and
bellows like a bear. Her eyes shift wildly.

He jumps back—stunned—then charges.

Except his legs flail in mid-air. Devere holds him by his collar.

"You?" Grouchy swings Honey-Stick her direction. "You're the
Queen? The miserable, ass-chewing Queen who hurt my Snow?"

"Snow?" Lox says. "What about Snow?"

Grouchy jabs his sword at the Queen. "This fumping wench
sent a hag to poison her—to put Snow in a cursed sleep."

"Foolish stump." The Queen sneers. "I didn't send the hag to
poison Snow. I *was* the hag."

Grouchy looks at the Queen's hand and visualizes it clutching
that damn apple. He thinks of Snow's bite. Crisp skin. Exposed flesh.

"Wait," Hays says. "If you're the Queen, are you saying that the
bear killed King Francis?"

"Idiot." Battson shakes his head.

Red flames ignite in Grouchy's belly. He kicks backward, correctly estimating the location of Devere's groin. The giant falls to one knee and releases him. He lands on both feet, ignores the spike of pain in his bad leg, and charges again at the Queen.

Just steps away from the foul witch, sharp teeth clamp around his already-wounded ankle and tear open the bearclaw laceration. He spills hard on his belly and kicks at Yanky, who whimpers and growls. Battson tries to pin Grouchy down, and Hays pulls off his dog.

Outside, a cacophony erupts—an all-too familiar mixture of stomping feet, hissing, and moaning. Everyone stops wrestling, groaning, or otherwise flailing. Rain drums upon the roof. Closest to the window, the miserable Queen approaches the glass.

She gasps and shakes her head.

Grouchy shoves Battson away and climbs off the floor. Together with the humans, he joins the Queen at the window.

Below, dozens—no, hundreds—of ghoulish villagers jostle together in the street. Most are the hissing hot variety, though some undead cold Horrors mill about as well. The hot Horrors scour the street, kick open doors, and head-butt windows.

The grotesqueness of the scene makes Grouchy's brain flip-flop in his skull. A staggering corpse missing a hand. A shirtless pregnant woman running through the streets, drool and blood dripping from her mouth. A young girl missing most of one cheek flailing in the mud. Exposed ribs. Demented children. Caked blood. Oozing wounds. Wild eyes. Torn skin. Ripped flesh.

Streamers and ribbons hang from the fronts of each building, and one massive banner proclaims:

VILLAGE OF ABUNDANCE
APPLE BUTTER FESTIVAL

Grouchy looks down. He remembers staring into the ravine and watching the hag fall, presumably to her death. Pain and loss chewed at his stomach, boiling over into rage. He'd kicked that apple as hard as he could. Juice and pulp rained into the air. The apple fell out of sight.

Now he's not at all surprised when the Queen whispers, "Tell me, stump, what did you do with the apple after I fell off the cliff?"

"I kicked the damn thing into the ravine." Grouchy's belly quivers. "Why, ass-muffin? Was that a bad thing?"

"Apparently so."

Below, hisses and moans drown out the falling rain. He can no longer see the muddy street, now eclipsed by countless thirsty eyes and ravenous mouths, a rising tide of torn skin and exposed flesh.

TO BE CONTINUED IN...

ACKNOWLEDGMENTS

ONCE UPON A TIME, my then four-year-old daughter and I watched Walt Disney's animated version of Snow White for probably the ninth or tenth time. You watch anything enough times, and you start to see the darkness simmering underneath. You make up your own backstory. You try to figure out why any halfway sensible young woman who was being pursued by dark forces would take an apple from a creepy stranger. You do this not to mock a classic tale, but to add depth to it—to give it even more meaning and make it fresh. You do it with respect, or at least that's what I've tried to do here.

I hope I've succeeded.

If I haven't, then it's in spite of the support, kindness, and partnership of a great many people. And it's to these people that I owe a great many thanks.

To the family.

A big thank-you and hug to my dad for seeing me through college and for passing along his love of dark fiction, and to my mom for always supporting my creativity. If you walk into either of my parent's homes, you'll see some of my childhood artwork framed on the wall. Being treated like an artist in this way has a profound impact on a child. Props to my sister for showing me that even cool kids read books. And hugs to my Uncle Darrel for buying me stacks of Hardy Boys books and introducing me to so much music. Loving thanks, too, to the memory of my Mammaw and Pappaw for always taking the time to make a rhyme.

To the teachers.

Especially to the English teachers, I owe a debt of gratitude for escorting me down this long path. Julie Johnson at Maumee High School gave me a list of words needing metaphors and provided me with an opportunity to shine. Don Dunstan at Greenon High School always embraced my inspiration no matter how bizarre. Nicole Macklin, formerly of Wright State's Writing Center, hired a goofball with a broken leg and put me in the company of many great writers. I owe bottomless thanks as well to the entire English Department at Wright State University, most especially Carol Loranger, Gary Pacernick, and Jimmy Chesire. Carol, you showed me how to think critically, even about the untouchable Batman. Gary, you expanded my definition of the word *poetry* now and forever. Jimmy, you praised the good and pointed out the bad—and always with kindness.

To the writers.

Over the course of three summers, Sharon Short and the many volunteers and staff at the Antioch Writers Workshop provided me with an unparalleled immersion into the craft of writing. Thank you to Ron Rollins and the staff at Dayton Daily News for establishing the Dayton Daily News/Antioch Writers' Workshop Short Story Contest, and to Rebecca Morean and the faculty at Sinclair Community College for holding their Annual Creative Writing Contest—both contests provided me with a scholarship to the Antioch Writers' Workshop, an amazing gift and opportunity. I also owe thanks to authors William Kent Krueger, Linda Gerber, Brady Allen, and Jeffrey Marks for taking a moment to share with me their thoughts, talents, and tips, and to Joy Levett for offerin' some helpful insights and advice in the final hours.

A big shout-out to Katrina Kittle for teaching me the importance of stoking tension and the value of chanting "Lemon Face, Lion Face." And to Jeffrey Ford for reminding me to take my hands off the wheel and for putting the key on the plate.

As well, this story would not exist without the Brothers Grimm and all the many writers since who have kept Snow White and her dwarfs alive in our imaginations. I'd highly recommend Philip Pullman's *Fairy Tales from the Brothers Grimm: A New English Version* to anyone interested in reading classic fairy tales and identifying some of the many Easter eggs hidden in this story.

On the topic of book recommendations, if you're looking for the most practical book on the craft of writing ever written, then you need look no further than *Hooked* by author Les Edgerton. Les is a damn good writer, a no-nonsense teacher, and an awesome friend. This piece would not have seen print without him. The next round is on me, Les.

To the publishers.

I owe a big thanks to Aaron Patterson and Kate Copsey at StoneHouse Ink for being so easy to work with and for helping my dream become a reality. Aaron, thank you for taking a chance on me. Kate, thank you for patiently responding to my endless questions. Where do you find the patience? See, I can't help myself, can I? Is there no end to my incessant questioning? I am thrilled to be working with you both on the next books. Thanks, too, to my editors Daniel Friend and Heather Moore for calling into question every fragment and for urging me to give this book a better ending.

To the readers.

In no particular order, my deepest thanks to Sarah Zettler, Elizabeth Nickell, Frank Smith, Kelley Ryan, Michelle Lee, Walter Boley, Tina Johnson, Kerry Castin, Tara Roberts, Susan Goodfellow, and Cynthia Marshall. With the exception of Frank and Walter, you are all beautiful, talented women. Thank you for taking the time to read the earlier drafts of this story and for offering your words of criticism, encouragement, and insight. Frank, I wish I'd listened to you sooner on a good many things. Sarah, thank you for the many hours spent with this book and for your delightfully blunt feedback. And extra special thanks to Cynthia for far more than I deserve.

To the inspiration.

To my daughter Annabella. Before you came into my life, I had no stories to tell. Then you showed up, and the fiction began to flow. You are a constant source of happiness and wonder. You make me a better writer, a better dad, and a better person overall. Thank you for your continued patience when I need to write just a few more words, for your beautiful smiles and your maniacal laughs, for your companionship through many adventures, and for not beating me up too badly during our karate fights.

Rob E. Boley
The Heart of It All
July 2013

ABOUT THE AUTHOR

ROB E. BOLEY GREW UP in Enon, Ohio, a little town with a big Indian mound. He later earned a B.A. and M.A. in English from Wright State University in Dayton, Ohio. His fiction has appeared in several markets, including *A cappella Zoo, Pseudopod, Necrotic Tissue, and Best New Werewolf Tales*. His stories have won Best in Show in the Sinclair Community College Creative Writing Contest (2013) and the Dayton Daily News/Antioch Writers' Workshop Short Story Contest (2012). He lives with his daughter in Dayton, where he works for his alma mater. Each morning and most nights, he enjoys making blank pages darker.

You can get to know him better online by visiting his website at www.robboley.com, liking his Facebook author page at www.facebook.com/RobBoleyAuthor, or following him on Twitter @robboley.

STONEGATE ink

Made in the USA
San Bernardino, CA
03 May 2014